POND SCUM

Alan Silberberg

HYPERION BOOKS
FOR CHILDREN

NEW YORK

First Edition

1 3 5 7 9 10 8 6 4 2

This book is set in 12-point Celestia Antiqua.

Designed by Christine Kettner

Printed in the United States of America

Reinforced binding

Library of Congress Cataloging-in-Publication Data on file.

ISBN 0-7868-5634-3

Visit www.hyperionbooksforchildren.com

For Kalie and Zach—
the light, the laughter, and loves of my life

A.S.

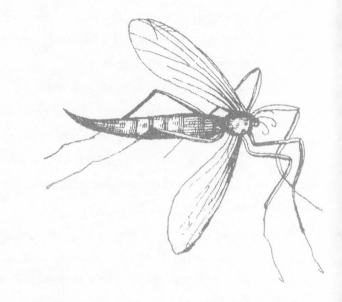

CHAPTER ONE

THE MOSQUITOES were toasting another victory. As proof of their job well done, a Volvo station wagon was speeding up the bumpy dirt road, filled with screaming kids swollen with bites the size of quarters. The FOR SALE sign still hung safely in front of the homely house at the end of No-way Way.

Three sneaky newts had to jump quickly to avoid the stomping shoes of Belinda Shrank, the real estate agent, who, for the fifth time this year, couldn't close the deal on this "three bedroom, one and a half bathroom, five acre, waterfront dream." Belinda pulled a jumbo-sized can of BugOut from her purse and sprayed a toxic cloud that followed her from the broken doorstep of the property to her minivan, cursing the bugs as she sprinted to safety.

She squeezed her wide body into the driver's seat, accompanied by an unseen milk snake, who quickly made itself at home around Belinda's ankle. Her scream was muffled by the tightly shut windows, which were splattered by an arsenal of bird poop. Had it not been for the fat raccoon clawing at the windshield like a masked mime, she might've driven away without smashing into the birch tree.

Just her luck.

Oliver was pulling the wings off another fly. His favorite part was the almost-silent *snap* of the transparent wing breaking off from the fat thorax. He could do this all day, and now that it was summer, it seemed that he was. He loved torturing the bugs that he stalked then sucked up with his mother's DustBuster. Only eleven, he already had a mean streak worthy of a seventeen-year-old, and his stocky, short build and wild tangle of brown weedlike hair only enhanced his bulldog demeanor.

With the exception of the bug carcasses scattered by the windowsill, Oliver's bedroom betrayed none of the anger and hurt that the boy carried with him like a second skin. It was a typical kid's room: dirty clothes lay scattered on the floor, and a Game Boy was abandoned on his messy desk. Intricate model airplanes kept company with worn stuffed animals.

He wasn't a bad kid—just a lonely boy who felt compelled to snatch the flies that kept him company.

Oliver's fascination with insects began as a hobby he'd started with his dad when he was eight. They would spend hours identifying and classifying the colorful beetles and scary-looking millipedes they'd stumbled across on their nightly GOOGLE searches. Together they'd made a scrapbook of material gathered on their sojourns into the bug-infested woods and jungles of cyberspace. But that was before the divorce, and now insects didn't interest him in quite the same way.

"You are seriously disturbed." It was Oliver's fourteen-year-old sister, Rachel, watching from the safety of the doorway, with her best friend, Cherise. She was always with her friend, which was just one of the reasons Oliver hated his sister so much.

"Buzz off," said Oliver as he tossed the flightless fly out the apartment window. Then he reached into the glass fish tank and trapped another slow-moving one in his hand. He sneered as he stared into the bug's compound eyes. "Flying is *so* overrated," he said as he pinched its flimsy wings. He smiled thinly, then pulled with the delight of a child opening a birthday party favor.

The sound was delicious.

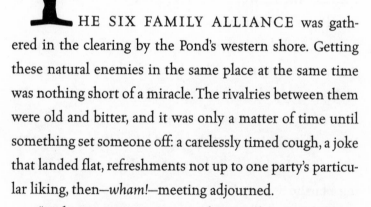

CHAPTER TWO

THE SIX FAMILY ALLIANCE was gathered in the clearing by the Pond's western shore. Getting these natural enemies in the same place at the same time was nothing short of a miracle. The rivalries between them were old and bitter, and it was only a matter of time until something set someone off: a carelessly timed cough, a joke that landed flat, refreshments not up to one party's particular liking, then—*wham!*—meeting adjourned.

"Welcome, Insects, Mammals, Reptiles, Amphibians, Birds, and Fish." This greeting came from Fat Mama, the large black widow spider who hung in her web surrounded by her arachnid kin.

A roaring whir of approval rose up from the Insect Elders, who had only recently voted the spider into power after an unfortunate run-in with a bicycle tire put an end to the stinkbug's reign. Though technically not insects, the spiders were considered part of the Insect clan, giving the smallest members of the Alliance a larger voting block.

"Once again, I remind everyone that Alliance rules dictate that this is strictly a 'snack-free' meeting."

Of the Six Family leaders, Fat Mama was the most straightforward speaker, which explained why she had won the right to be the head of the entire Alliance, a position she held with authority.

"Rules, shmules, it's a frog-eat-bug world," croaked Frankie "The Tongue" Gambini, the slobbering bullfrog kingpin of the Amphibians. He gave the nearest ladybug the evil eye, then shot out his sticky tongue. Thankfully for the ladybug, Frankie's eyesight wasn't what it used to be, and he ended up with an acorn in his stomach.

"Please, can we just get this thing done? I got some unfinished business with a garbage can." The request came from the head of the Mammals, a pudgy raccoon aptly named Pudge.

"You tell 'em, Pudge," added Hinky, the one-eyed skunk by his side, who lifted his tail just enough to make the others flinch. "Come on, gimme a reason to blast ya. I will, you know."

"Ffffft!" The gassy sound didn't come from the skunk, but from Frankie. "What? It wasn't me," protested the fat frog as the others coughed and gagged with disgust. The meeting was off to a smelly start.

Out of nowhere, a rock landed on the leader of the Reptile Family, an opinionated box turtle whose chronic dry skin had earned him the nickname "Flakes." Annoyed, the turtle glanced skyward before muttering, "I hate crows."

Twenty feet above, a flock of crows cackled as their chevron formation circled the assembly on the ground. "That's getting their attention, huh, General?" piped up Antoine, the scrawniest member of the elite Black Angels squadron.

Eduardo Ignacio Santo Domingo, the largest, sleekest crow, and distinguished head of the Bird family, smacked Antoine in the head. "You idiot! This is supposed to be a peaceful mission."

"Oopsies." Antoine was always making mistakes, both big and small, and if he weren't General Santo Domingo's nephew, he'd be flying with the garbage crew instead of the famous Black Angels.

The General and his crow cadets swooped fast and low over the meeting, forcing everyone to quickly duck (except the ducks, who just jumped back into the pond with a loud splash).

Much to the impatience of the other birds who'd elected him, The General and his crew finally landed. Finches flinched. Swallows gulped. But as usual, no one said a word, because if you valued your feathers, you didn't mess with The General.

Born in the nearby woods, he was a distant descendant of the Tamaulipas breed of crows from Mexico. Some said that was why The General was so full of himself: because his blood flowed from such a distinguished lineage.

"So? I hear we had another close call today." The crow eyed the spider closely as he took his position around the large flat rock that served as the Alliance bargaining table. "I hope you intend to strengthen your position *this time.*"

Fat Mama was used to The General's surly attitude. She knew that he hated the humans only slightly more than he hated her. "Now that The General has kindly graced us with his presence," the spider said, turning away from his steady gaze, "let us get down to business."

"Antoine! *Scram!*" The General shouted to his nephew. "Go get lost in the woods."

The small crow nodded, then walked off into the twisted knot of trees and rocks that surrounded the Pond. Getting lost was something he was actually good at.

As always, the Alliance meeting was "Elders Only," meaning, no kids allowed. The grown-ups had determined long ago that kids only got in the way, with their silly ideas and sillier questions, which is why Pond decisions were made by adults.

"It kills me that the stupid Elders won't even let us listen."

The whisper came from an unseen voice within the tall cotton grass by the edge of the water. Slowly, a pair of round, compound eyes poked through the stalks, staring intently in the direction of the meeting. Even though he knew better, Willy, a fast, young dragonfly with a wild blue streak down his back, ached to fly over and give them all a piece of his mind.

Willy continued his quiet tirade. "I'm telling ya, listening to an adult is like listening to—"

"Zzzzzzz." The dragonfly's speech was cut short by the ferocious snore of a plump spotted salamander, fast asleep in the soft marshy moss.

"Mooch! Wake up! This is important!"

The salamander squinted and yawned. His dark skin was moist, giving the dozen or so yellow spots along his body a soft glow. Opening his mouth, his first statement, as always, was the same: "I'm hungry."

Willy had to laugh. If there was one constant around the Pond, it was Mooch's appetite.

"It is with sincere gratitude that I address you all." Fat

Mama paused to allow the beaver to translate her words for those hard-of-breathing members of the Alliance. The beaver stuck his head underwater and repeated everything to the anxious Fish below, who were uncomfortable—not because of what was being discussed—they simply hoped that the beaver wasn't hungry. Otherwise, the longer the speech went on above, the fewer would last below.

"Once again, our combined efforts have worked marvelously to keep the humans away." The spider was referring to the recent group attack by bug, bird, reptile, and mammal to chase off the potential buyers of the little house.

The Pond erupted in a chorus of enthusiastic chirps, buzzes, croaks, and caws. Thanks to the goal of keeping human hands away from the purity of the Pond, all species were acting as one—natural rivalries put aside for the good of them all.

"What is it with these Elders?" asked Willy, annoyed at what he'd just heard. He'd been listening to this sort of anti-human talk since he was practically a larva, and frankly, he was sick of it. He was bursting to speak with the Alliance—something he tried to do with any Pond Elder who crossed his path—but being just a kid, they always made it clear his opinions were not welcome. "Come on," Willy would explain, "you're blowing it big time. Humans might be a good thing!"

The Elders' response was always the same. They

listened. They nodded. And then, once the dragonfly finished his impassioned plea, they said, "Shut up, Willy."

Which is why Willy felt that his greatest threat in life wasn't ending up as someone's breakfast or squashed against the windshield of an unseen car; it was dealing with the Elders' small-minded ideas. "Maybe that house isn't supposed to stay empty. Did they ever think of that? I don't think so. Just cuz they're *adults*—they think they know everything. Well, I'll tell ya, Mooch—they don't!"

As usual, the salamander wasn't really listening. He was too busy trying to snack on a small worm without Willy noticing. They had an agreement: Mooch promised not to eat any buzzing, flying, or crawling things when his dragonfly friend was around. But he was famished. And besides, it was just *one* worm.

"What do you say, buddy? Let's sneak in and give them a piece of our minds. I haven't gotten booted out of an Alliance meeting for a whole month!" Willy turned just in time to catch Mooch slurping down the last bit of his snack like a long strand of spaghetti.

Sllllllrp!

"Mooch! You promised," exploded Willy. "How will I ever know you won't eat me? Huh? Don't I look good? Wouldn't I be yummy?"

Mooch secretly had to admit that, yes, dragonflies do taste good; but he knew better than to say anything.

Instead, he simply shrugged and told Willy that he was perfectly able to control his hunger, and more important, friends just aren't appetizing.

Willy was angry. Angry with Mooch. Angry with being shut out of another stupid Alliance meeting. "You do what you have to. I'm gonna blow off some steam and fly a few laps around the Pond or something," he said before soaring off, leaving Mooch to finish his treat alone.

"Oh, man. I did it again" was all a guilty Mooch could say before foraging in the dirt for a second, third, and fourth slimy course.

CHAPTER THREE

BESIDE PULLING WINGS off flies, summer vacation meant one thing to Oliver: TV. No matter what his mother did to wean him from his channel-changing addiction, the television always triumphed.

His mom tried everything. Rationing his viewing time backfired when he used his "TV tokens" to choose only violent, disgusting shows. She made him go to a summer camp where he promptly came down with a mysterious rash and had to be sent home. His mother even did the unthinkable—had the cable turned off completely. But when Oliver's hunger strike reached day three, she thought it medically wrong not to call the cable company and reinstate service, and even added HBO, to "fatten him back up."

For Oliver, being able to guilt his parents into getting his way was the only positive result of the divorce. He found that a pouting face went farther now, and both his mother and father were easy prey for his quivering lower lip. He didn't want much—just to be left alone to watch TV and have enough money to keep his junk-food drawer full. Of course, he got less mileage out of his father, which had more to do with his dad's obsession with work than any condition of the divorce.

Arthur Durkin, Oliver's dad, was the research director at BioProthesis Inc., a manufacturer of synthetic body parts and limbs. When Oliver was younger, it had totally creeped him out, and he had told kids that his father was a plumber. But now that he was in middle school he delighted in telling wide-eyed classmates the stories of his visits to the factory where fake hands and plastic kneecaps were strung from racks like an assortment of hats, or sausages in a butcher's window.

Oliver's mom, Carol Thurman (she'd taken back her maiden name over the protests of the kids), hadn't worked outside the home since Rachel was born. Oliver knew she used to be a high school science teacher, but that was just one of those historical family facts that didn't have much relevance to his life. The idea of his mother with a *real job* was as foreign to him as one of those Italian movies he stumbled across on late-night television. And as long as he could channel surf his days away, he could ignore his mother's struggle to make ends meet on the check his dad sent every month. It was so easy. With the push of the power button, Oliver could immerse himself in the fantasy lives of cartoon or sitcom characters and avoid thinking about the changes the divorce had already made in his life—or the inevitable changes to come.

So it was a shock the day that the first big change *did* come. He was watching a Bugs Bunny cartoon when he heard the scream.

"Ahhhhhhhhhhhh!"

It was loud. It was piercing. It was his mother. Oliver actually turned off the TV and ran into the kitchen, half expecting to find a maniac holding a machete to her throat, or some awful leg-twisted-like-a-pretzel injury. Which is why, when he saw her just crying uncontrollably at the kitchen table, he was confused and a little let down.

"Gee, Mom. Not again." Oliver figured it was just another weepy post-divorce breakdown. They were happening less and less this past year—which was fine by him. He never knew what he should say or do, and usually just retreated back to the fortress of his room.

But as she turned to look at him, Oliver knew something was different. She was smiling. Her wet cheeks made those funny dimples he liked, as she wiped the tears with a piece of paper that had a strange letterhead on top.

"Ollie. Honey. Guess what?" she said as she stood up to show him the letter. "I got a job. We're moving."

CHAPTER FOUR

"YOU WHAT?"

Mooch had never seen Willy's wings vibrate so furiously. The salamander took a step back before trying to explain. "It was an accident. I swear." Mooch's skin began secreting a sticky mucus, as it always did when he was feeling nervous or uneasy. Best friends often fight, and usually once the steam blows over, they patch things up and move forward like nothing had ever happened. But this was different. Mooch's secret had been discovered and Willy was beyond mad.

16

"I don't care *how* it happened, Mooch. You broke your promise. You ate my cousin. As a *snack!*"

Mooch looked down at the ground, ashamed of what he'd done. There was nothing wrong with a salamander eating a dragonfly. It happened every day. It's *supposed* to happen. But he hadn't honored his agreement with Willy. The food chain was one thing, but their friendship was supposed to come first.

"Look, I don't think I can hang out with you anymore," Willy said, staring down at Mooch. "I just can't take the chance."

"But, Willy," Mooch pleaded. "We're best friends."

"Really?" Willy shot back. "Not anymore."

And then the dragonfly was gone. His sleek body darted off and was quickly lost in a sea of sky-blue forget-me-nots.

Mooch couldn't get that awful confrontation out of his mind. It had been a whole week without Willy, and he still felt terrible about losing a friend. He hated how his appetite kept getting in the way of his social life. He'd eaten six of his seven friends in the past year.

Mooch had known Willy forever, and now the loneliness was overwhelming. Who would he chase fireflies with? Who else would have as much fun playing practical jokes on the blue jays? And without Willy, who would be Mooch's undercover partner when he wanted to secretly explore the Forbidden Zone on the other side of the pavement? That was where *they* lived—the humans—and both Mooch and Willy were fascinated with the odd, upright species. Together, they would sneak into town and study human nature up close, mesmerized by the colors, sounds, smells—and for Mooch—the delicious snacks!

"I don't get it," Mooch remembered saying on their last covert visit to town. "Why is everyone back home so down on people? They don't look too bad to me." They were in a park, watching two kids chase each other around a sandbox while their mother shouted to be careful and to take their fingers out of their noses. "Kids play. Adults yell. It's the same at the Pond, isn't it?"

Willy landed by Mooch's side. "Yeah. But the Pond grown-ups yell because they're scared all the time. You gotta understand, the Alliance is totally freaked out by anything human. They think all humans are exactly the same— *bad*. And once they make up their minds about something, trust me, that's it."

That's it. With their friendship now over, those words resonated for Mooch. Willy would never admit it, but he was that way too. Sure, Mooch had broken a promise, but Willy was the one who had made up his mind, and that was *it* for the friendship.

Mooch trudged through the wet grass on his way to nowhere in particular. Summer was the best time of year at the Pond, but now, without his best friend, it was turning into the worst.

"Quiet! Someone's comin'."

Mooch stopped. Looking around to where he thought he'd heard the voices, he realized that he had wandered into the thick weedy spot near the mouth of the little stream that fed the Pond. He didn't know this area well. He wasn't scared or anything, he was just aware that he had entered unfamiliar territory, someone else's playground, perhaps. Mooch listened carefully—not moving—hoping to fool whoever or whatever it was into thinking that he'd gone.

Standing still by the stream, the late afternoon sun felt nice against his back. Trying not to move had a hypnotic effect, and it wasn't long before the buzzing cicadas had lulled Mooch into a nap. He had nowhere to be and no one to be with, so he sank into the cool corner of a shaded rock and fell into a nice dreamy place—where he was friends with everyone, no matter how good they tasted.

The crescent-shaped moon rose and hung low in the summer sky. Fireflies played tag and hide-and-seek with the other bugs, making the field by the Pond sparkle and sing.

Mooch opened his eyes. The darkness startled him at first and it took him a moment to remember where he was—that he'd heard some strange voices, and that his friendship with Willy was really over. He stretched his slithery body and climbed atop the still-warm rock he'd been sleeping under. I should probably get home, he thought, knowing how his mother always worried.

He turned to head back the way he'd come—and was shocked to see six little spiders blocking his way, dangling from threads that clung to the tree branches above. They were just kids, but they stared back at him with a fierceness that, quite honestly, gave him a chill.

"Not to worry, kiddos," he joked nervously. "I make it a personal policy not to eat anyone younger than me, okay?"

They didn't smile. They didn't blink. They simply dropped to the ground, stepped forward (all forty-eight spindly legs), and yelled out: "Spy!" And before Mooch had a chance to laugh at the accusation, they covered him in silken webs that stuck to him like glue.

"Hey! Didn't your mothers tell you not to play with loaded spinnerets?" he said with a shaky laugh.

But the spiders didn't say anything. They just stared back and then disappeared into the dark trees, leaving Mooch to worry that this was not just a silly children's game.

He twisted and arched his back, but soon realized he was making the situation worse. The sticky silk began to dry and contract, and soon he was trapped in a cocoon that left little room for him to breathe. He began to panic, but his calls for help mixed into the swelling buzz and din of the dusk, and for the first time, the grim reality of the situation settled in on him. He was hungry.

And if he was hungry, so was someone else—someone bigger and with a stronger foothold on the food chain. It seemed that it would be just a matter of time before a gluttonous beaver or famished fox stumbled upon him—a plump, pre-wrapped salamander snack.

Mooch closed his eyes tightly and imagined his demise. Would whoever made a meal of him go slowly, limb by limb? Or would they just gobble him down in one ravenous bite? He wondered if it would hurt to be chewed up, swallowed, then digested. Oddly, he'd never given the matter a single thought when he was the eat-er, but as eat-ee, things certainly took on a different flavor.

"Come on, Hesh, put some muscle into it!" The voice, vibrating and low, seemed to be coming from inside him. Mooch felt himself hoisted ever so slightly off the ground, which made him worry that he was already dead and this was his ascension to heaven, where bugs and animals lived happily together without worry or hunger pangs.

"Heave! Ho!" the voice called out from under him. Then with a sudden lurch forward, Mooch realized he was moving.

"Listen, you, I don't want no trouble. You got me?" It was that voice again. But this time it seemed to be coming from a different place. A place *on* him.

"You strayed into the wrong neck of the woods, pal," the voice continued. "Don't pull no tricks and I won't inflict no pain."

Mooch had to squint to try and see who it was. And only after he crossed his eyes was he finally able to focus and see an ant standing on his nose; a tiny, tough, red ant who, like the spiders, was just a kid.

"Who are you? What's going on here?" Mooch asked, more scared than curious.

In response, the red ant bit down hard on his nose. "No talking! And that's an order! You got me?"

Mooch's nose throbbed with hot pain, but he dared not scream. The fierce young ant poked at his face and bounced up and down on some of the puffy skin around his cheeks. "I got forty-five of my best ants under you. I figured I only needed thirty, but you're a fat boy, aren't ya?"

"I'm big boned," Mooch replied defensively before feeling the searing pain of the ant's bite again.

"I said no talking!" The ant then leaned over and screamed, "Come on, Hesh, you're not pulling ten times your weight!"

And with that, the tough red ant settled confidently atop Mooch's brow, the captain of a salamander ship on a voyage to who-knows-where.

Mooch was living a nightmare. Tied up, a prisoner of tiny deranged ants, he was now being carried upside down into a part of the woods he'd never seen before. Prickly bull thistle spines poked against his sides, and the sweet smell of lilacs and night-blooming jasmine filled his nostrils.

After a few more minutes, the red ant stood up and

started barking out directions to his army below. "Ten paces to the right! Twenty paces down the embankment! Through the clover and we're there!"

"There." The word echoed ominously in Mooch's mind. He imagined the "there" where he would meet his end. He pictured the worst. Sharp teeth. Heavy, brain-crushing rocks. But when the ant entourage came to an abrupt halt and dumped him in a small strange clearing, Mooch was shocked to see that he was surrounded by an assembly of bugs—young bugs—watching him with curious eyes.

"Untie the intruder!" called out an unseen-yet-vaguely-familiar voice. A swarm of bees encircled Mooch, their stingers deftly poking at and breaking apart the silk bonds. Mooch was free, and he puffed out his belly. "Ahhhhhh," he sighed, feeling his wide girth fill with each deep breath.

"Gee, guys, it's been swell," began Mooch, slowly backing out of the center of the circle, hoping he'd soon be able to make a break for the woods. But when his six spider captors suddenly dropped from a low branch and blocked his exit, he changed his mind.

Mooch inched back into the center of the circle. The sound of whirring wings filled his ears, making his head swim. Out of the cacophony he was able to make out a slow soft chant, which started quietly, but soon, as the voices joined together, reached a fever pitch.

"Spy! Spy! Spy! Spy!"

Mooch trembled at this incantation. What had he

done? Why was he here? His head ached and he felt like he needed to puke. He feared this was truly the end. But then the chanting stopped suddenly, and the only sound he heard was his own tiny heart beating a mile a minute.

Mooch looked up to see the circle breaking, the insects clearing a path. For one dumb second he thought they were making way for his escape. But that hope was dashed when he saw who entered the circle.

It was Willy.

CHAPTER FIVE

THE VAN TURNED a sharp corner onto a narrow tree-lined street that contained the soul of the small town: a drugstore, a hardware store, and a diner. "Here ya go," Belinda Shrank announced from the driver's seat. "Main Street, Little Falls."

Oliver took his nose out of his Game Boy and looked at the view. "Oh, great," was all the enthusiasm he could muster.

"I don't care if I have to live in a cardboard box and sleep outside your building." His sister was on the phone with her best friend, Cherise. "My mother can't make me move to this dump."

"Yes, she can," a voice replied calmly from the front seat of the minivan.

Oliver watched as Rachel gave their mom *the look*: eyes narrowed like venetian blinds and scowling tight fish lips. After holding her dramatic pose, his sister gave up, tossed the cell phone inside her shoulder bag, and went back to sulking.

Despite the lack of enthusiasm in the backseat, Belinda Shrank continued her realtor ramblings up in front. "And we turn left onto Grand Avenue, which isn't grand enough to be an avenue, but it is home to—"

"A movie theater? An arcade? McDonald's?" asked Oliver, hopeful that somewhere there'd be a sign of civilization as he knew it.

"Nope," said Belinda. "Home to the Shranks. Gotta grab my keys. Be back in a jiff."

She slammed on the brakes, and the van stopped short in front of a large Victorian house that had probably been beautiful about a zillion years ago. The wraparound front porch sagged like an old lady's spine. Half the shutters were missing. And several different paint jobs had been begun and abandoned over the years: there was a lime green porch that clashed with the brown and yellow siding, and the second story clapboards were striped red and blue.

"Home, creepy home," Rachel said, once Belinda

disappeared inside. "You really want to find a place to live from *her?*"

"Want to? No. Have to? Yes," said their mother. "She's the only real estate agent here. Besides, Mrs. Shrank sounded so excited on the phone." Carol turned around and beamed at her children. "She said she's got the perfect place for us. Not an apartment. Not a condo. A HOUSE!"

Oliver and Rachel looked at each other. They knew that tone of voice. Their mother was in her *happy* place, where she was envisioning their lives finally becoming something out of one of the many *Home and Whatever* magazines that lay scattered in their apartment bathroom. To their mom, a house meant normal. A house meant family. A house meant homemade curtains, and cookies in the oven, a fresh-baked smell in the air.

Belinda swung her wide hips back into the van, jingling a ring of keys. "This is your lucky day!" she said a little too brightly before shifting into reverse and screeching off toward No-way Way.

Hinky wasn't always a miserable one-eyed skunk. He used to be a miserable two-eyed skunk. Contrary to what the others said, the accident that cost him an eye didn't make him bitter; it only justified his sour outlook on life, forever marking his personality.

He knew he was deformed and scary looking. He even liked it. What he didn't like was *them*—the humans. He could barely utter the word, let alone contain his scent glands from leaking involuntarily whenever one of them was near.

It was their fault he only saw half of the world—the half that was filled with hate. As a child he'd wandered into a human campsite, drawn by the glowing fire and strange smells. Everyone at the Pond knew his story—how he'd fought off the evil man who, for no reason, attacked him with a knife. But no one knew the truth—that he'd actually burned his eye getting too close to a gooey marshmallow impaled on a red-hot stick.

It was his turn to be Watcher. The Six Families rotated the duty. Each day, someone from one of the groups had to be positioned near the head of the dirt road, to keep an eye open for intruders.

The skunk paced back and forth. Because of his limited field of vision, he had to be in constant motion in order to see the entire wide road. "Left. Right. Back. Forth. This is boring. I hate my job."

Hinky felt that sentry work was beneath him. But he did as he was told. His loyalty to Pudge was strong. After all, the raccoon had befriended him when the pain of his accident was fresh and the other animals were giving him the cold shoulder for being such a freak.

The sound of tires on gravel snapped him to attention. He had to swirl his head all the way around to see what the noise was about. His nose sniffed the air cautiously. And then his eye went wide with fear. He did everything his body told him to do—except for one thing: move out of the middle of the road.

Belinda drove nervously. She appeared to be agitated about something, and Oliver was sure this woman was seriously disturbed. The van bounced and jerked along the dirt road like an amusement park ride. He watched as tree branches and pebbles hit the windshield, and for a moment imagined he was on a real adventure, not just some stupid house-hunting mission.

The van continued down the road. Hinky still couldn't move. But he *could* scream. "Code Red! Code Red!" he shouted as he lifted his tail and a foul odor filled the air. His good eye closed as the van came straight at him, filling his field of vision and ensuring his untimely demise.

The Pond Alliance Emergency System was pretty simple: Code Green—Friendly Visitor. Code Blue—Animal Intruder. Code Yellow—Human Intruder. Code Red— Belinda Shrank.

Oliver watched as Belinda gripped the wheel so tight the skin at her knuckles was white. "So," asked the real estate agent in a voice higher than normal. "What do you think so far?"

And though it was in all their minds, Oliver said it first, "I *think* I smell a skunk!"

* * *

Hinky lay in the middle of the road, curled in a stunned and stinky ball. He wasn't moving. He wasn't breathing. But he wasn't dead. The van had rocked and bumped and roared right over him, and if he had been a little taller or the road a little smoother, he'd definitely be on a one-eyed, one-way trip to skunk heaven. But there he was. Alive and filled with even more hatred for humans than ever.

As soon as he made sure that all his limbs were functioning, he ran toward the woods, shouting, "Code Red! She's back! Code Red!"

"You're kidding, right?" Oliver was shocked at the first sight of his potential new home. It had to be a joke.

The van sat idling about fifteen yards from the broken-down property. To call it a "house" would be giving it too much credit. The two-story structure stood crooked and cracked, leaning to the left as if it had a broken hip. Several windows were busted or missing altogether. The roof sagged, the chimney tilted, and the old wooden exterior had been patched with even older wood, giving the term "rustic" a whole new meaning.

It sat back about fifty yards from a mongrel grove of pine, maple, and birch trees; the grass grew like weeds (or was it the weeds that grew like grass?); and even the flowers seemed to want to be somewhere else. Still, there was a pond, bright and sparkling, about a stone's throw away.

Belinda had finally loosened her death grip on the

wheel, but her eyes darted nervously, as if she were expecting something dreadful, which—given her past experience showing the house—was almost a sure thing.

Once, wasps had built a hidden nest inside the toilet bowl, which the prospective buyer discovered the hard way.

Another time, five raccoons (a younger and thinner Pudge among them) leaped from a bedroom closet, with sharp teeth bared, turning twin eleven-year-old brats into wailing puddles of tears.

Of course, the most revolting surprise Belinda had stumbled upon was the mountain of animal poop the size of a sofa. It took nine gallons of bleach and disinfectant to make the house smell even close to bearable.

"What do ya say, folks?" Belinda said with desperate enthusiasm. "Don't ya want to mosey inside?"

Oliver and Rachel watched their mother practically prance to the front porch.

"Come on, you two," their mom called back. "I'm going to get the best bedroom!"

"She's insane," Rachel said to her brother.

"Maybe," he replied. "But this van still stinks like a skunk!" Oliver pushed his way around his sister and bolted out the door.

Rachel sighed and then slid across the backseat. "Wait up, dweeb," she called to Oliver.

Belinda sat in the van, watching for any sign of trouble. *If the lady doesn't run out of the house in tears, or those* kids don't erupt in bee bites, she thought, then maybe it'll be okay this time.

She closed her eyes and counted to twenty-five. Then, Belinda Shrank dragged herself, out of the van, took one deep breath, and plastered the brightest smile she could on her face.

"Ready or not," she yelled, "here I come!"

CHAPTER SIX

"IT IS WAY GREAT to hang out again." Mooch was so excited, he was practically molting out of his skin. "And one more time, I promise never to eat another dragonfly, whether it's related to you or not."

Willy darted over their moss-covered hideout beneath the maple tree to make sure they were alone. Satisfied, he landed on the ground beside Mooch.

"You'd better watch what you eat," said Willy with a bit of edge in his voice. "Or next time maybe *you'll* end up dessert."

"Me?" Mooch said. "But dragonflies don't eat salamanders."

"No. But I've got a lot of hungry friends higher up the food chain who'd do me a favor." Willy was smiling now, and Mooch took his friend's wink to mean he wasn't angry anymore.

The truth was, Willy had missed having Mooch around, too. He was miserable the week they were apart, and Willy had come to the conclusion that an unpredictable friend is better than no friend at all.

"But this is the last time, Mooch." Willy's smile faded. He was serious. "One more mess-up and it's over between us. Understood?"

Though Mooch felt happy again, he was bursting to tell someone about the strange events that led to his reconciliation with Willy. But he'd promised the insects—sworn on a stack of mint leaves—that what he'd accidentally discovered would remain a secret.

It was amazing. First he was captured and brought into that circle of bugs, and then, there was Willy—his best friend whom he thought he'd never see again—and he was the head of his own secret alliance, the Alliance of Insect Kids!

"Let the intruder go," Willy's voice had called to the others that night. "He means us no harm."

"But Willy, you said *insects only* in our Kid Alliance," said a tough viceroy caterpillar named Gert. "What if he squeals? What if he ruins our plans?"

The other kids echoed her feeling. Mooch had wandered too close to their secret camp. He'd found out about them and could easily find out about their covert plan to sabotage the Alliance's next attempt to chase the humans away. If this salamander blabbed, all their hard work would be for nothing.

Mooch had watched in fear, and then awe, at the power Willy had over the others. He heard Willy's wings hum as he rose up into the center of the circle, looking down at the insect gathering.

"The salamander will not disrupt our goal," shouted Willy. "My word is the law. Unless anyone here wants to challenge it." His tone was harsh, and Mooch remembered how the other bugs immediately backed down. It was clear that Willy was calling the shots and no one dared stop him.

"By the way," Mooch began as he dug at the moss, aware that he had to hold himself back from grabbing a grub for a midmorning treat. "Thanks for, you know, sticking up for me that night."

"It was either that or stand back and watch you get covered in bee and wasp stings. Not a pretty sight. Or feeling!"

"They really woulda done that? Hurt me?"

"If I had told them to." Willy was proud of his own power. "You're the only one who knows what we're up to, Mooch. No matter what it takes—we will stop the Elders from keeping humans away. I have to be able to trust you on this. For real."

"Not a word. To anyone," Mooch promised. He meant it too—or at least hoped he did. "Do you really believe all that stuff—that kid insects could be leaders? About making friends with the humans?"

Willy sat on his bulbous backside. "Someone's got to believe that all humans aren't out to kill us. Lumping them together is as bad as saying all kids are weak and stupid." Willy's eyes looked past Mooch into some place only he could see. "When the time is right, we will make our move against the Alliance. It is our destiny to change things. To have our own voice."

Willy became different when he talked about this stuff. It was like someone else lived inside him and spoke using his mouth. "You'll see. Us kids will do this! We will make it happen!"

"Yeah, we will," said Mooch, grinning, even though he didn't really believe a word of it. Making friends with humans was suicide. And how could the insects, *kid insects* change things? They were the lowest rung of the food chain. They had the least real power. Willy's plan sounded good, and the memory of that night was still amazing, but truthfully, Mooch felt it was all kind of ridiculous.

"Code Red! Code Red!" Hinky's cry rang out as he ran through the thick woods, tripping over rocks and roots.

High up in a maple tree, Lester Biggs, a lethargic red-bellied woodpecker, heard the skunk's call and grudgingly went to work spreading the alarm.

"Great. As if I didn't already have a killer headache," the woodpecker said sourly while banging his bill again and again into the hard wood of the tree. Tap. "Ouch!" Tap-tap. "Oww!" Tap-tap-tap. "Oh, why couldn't I have been born a sparrow?"

The staccato beat echoed through the woods, sending its coded message. No one reacted faster than the two friends whose secret hideout was inside the base of that very wood-pecked tree.

"Shh. It's a warning!" cried Willy. "I think it's important."

Mooch had no idea what the message meant. He had never cared very much about the inner workings of the Pond, and had skipped all his code lessons in favor of playing or hunting down crunchy, gooey things to eat.

"What do you think it means, Willy?"

"Dunno for sure." Willy said. "But sounds like this could be 'it.'"

And though Mooch wasn't at all sure what "it" was, Willy hadn't looked this excited in a long time. And that made Mooch smile.

The Alliance Elders had gathered quickly at the flat rock. The spider. The crow. The raccoon. The turtle. The frog.

(The beaver was present, as always, to carry needed information to and from the trout.)

"How bad is it this time?" Fat Mama asked with an official, if slightly irritated, air. Hinky had the reputation for overreacting when he was on Watch duty.

Hinky flung himself to the ground below her, rolled his eye, and groaned, "It's Her. Do you hear me? Her!!"

"Yes, yes, yes. The round human who shrieks," croaked the fat frog. "She always shows up, and we always make her go away. What's the big deal?"

"The big deal is we need to be vigilant," said Pudge, who had come to Hinky's side. "If my man here says it's a problem, then I say—"

"You say? Since when do you carry the weight of a 'say'?" It was General Santo Domingo, and he was not smiling. "Need I remind you, Pudge, you're still on probation." The crow rose up on his talons and glared at the raccoon.

Pudge stared back at the General. For a moment, hatred beamed from behind his masked eyes. But it was true. He was still carrying around the weight of a catastrophically bad decision he'd made a short year ago.

It had seemed like a great idea at the time, an idea he had fought for. Pudge had single-handedly put into motion a mission to cross the Pavement and go into the Forbidden Zone to search for new sources of food and water. But there was no water, no food. And worse, they'd lost three good field mice that day to a bread delivery truck. The guilt and shame still clung to him with the acrid smell of failure (mixed with the aroma of freshly baked bread).

"I'm sure there's nothing to worry about," Fat Mama said, putting a halt to the staring match between Pudge and The General. "But let's err on the side of caution and send in the Angels."

The General nodded in agreement and quickly flew off, his raw cackling call rousing his feathered flyers to attention.

Meanwhile, on the other side of the Pond, Willy was flying toward the house and Mooch was having a very hard time keeping up.

"Dude, slow down!" pleaded Mooch.

But Willy's head was filled with images of a plan whose shape was becoming more and more real as he called out to his insect followers, "It's time! It's time! It's time!!"

Mooch was astonished as the earth seemed to burst alive with young insects crawling out from under rocks and dropping down from branches and hidden bushes. Moths. Mosquitoes. Centipedes. Beetles of every shape and color. All began a steady march in the same direction, trailing behind Willy, who flew on farther and farther ahead, leading this enormous army of kids.

"Onward! We will not be stopped, but we will stop *them!*" Willy shouted.

"Willy, what do I do?" called Mooch, feeling left out

and burdened by his weight (and species). But his best friend was lost to a cause that didn't include him, and Mooch did the only thing he could think of: follow the trail of bugs, heading someplace that was destined to change his life.

And for once, whether he'd live or die, eat or be eaten, didn't seem to matter, because Mooch sensed something that he couldn't explain. Something big was about to happen, and he knew only one thing: he had to be part of it.

CHAPTER SEVEN

FROM THE AIR, the Pond looked like a shiny golden eye staring up at the sun. Which is why flapping his wings high above it always gave Antoine the feeling that he was being watched. When he was just a baby crow, he and his mother (the honored sister of General Eduardo Ignacio Santo Domingo) would circle the Pond for hours; his mom singing songs, telling him stories, and sharing with him facts about life. Antoine's mother was sweet and funny and had the melodious voice of a songbird in the scruffy body of a crow.

Antoine missed his mother more and more, but his uncle was always telling him he had to be tough if he wanted to make it as a Black Angel. Crybaby tears wouldn't help promote him through the ranks. And if Antoine thought that his uncle would make it easy for him just because his mother was dead, he had another thing coming. If anything, The General was always pushing him, always riding his tail feathers, and trying to turn even his smallest victories into blemishes on his military record.

It wasn't that Antoine didn't feel grateful for his uncle's attention, he just wished he could be treated like the other recruits—catch even just a *little* slack.

"On my count. This is not, I repeat NOT, a drill." The General swooped in and out of the hovering squadron. "Now, you all know what do. Correct?"

"Yes, sir!" the young crows shouted back. The General, looking pleased with the answer, flew over to his nephew, who was, as always, bringing up the rear.

"Antoine, no mistakes. Understood?"

"Yes, sir. Uncle General, sir," gulped Antoine, thankful that no one saw how nervous he truly was. Nobody except a tough, mean cadet named Shadow.

"Hey, Antoine," Shadow called out as he knocked the smaller crow out of formation. "How's it feel to be such a loser?"

Antoine wanted desperately to say something back,

but as usual, he just held it all in and did his best to stay focused on the one thought that was his constant companion when he was around his uncle: don't mess up.

The house was scary. The floors were slanted like skateboard ramps. The walls were littered with holes. And the screens on the windows were all slashed and ripped, making the place an open invitation for intruders to come and go as they pleased.

Rachel was not an outdoorsy girl. And Oliver preferred the safety of a bag of cookies to the wilds of the woods. But their mother loved being in fresh air and had always hoped to live in the country someday. She was in heaven.

"Isn't this amazing, kids?" she asked, looking out a broken window at the light dancing on the pond.

"*Amazing* wasn't quite the word I was searching for," snapped Rachel as a foul odor she couldn't define caught her attention.

Off in the corner, Oliver had found an old chair and, out of habit, ignored everything. His nose was in his Game Boy, where pale invaders were being zapped into battery-operated dust.

"Yeah. Great. Whatever," he mumbled as he annihilated a spaceship with the flick of his thumb.

A fly buzzed tantalizingly around his head and then flew off before Oliver could snatch it. Shooting out of his reach, the fly headed straight toward the front door that Belinda Shrank was opening.

"Not again!" Belinda screamed, as the fly bounced repeatedly off her huge forehead before buzzing off into the daylight. For the umpteenth time that morning, Belinda reminded herself how desperately she wanted—no, *needed*—to sell this house.

"Well now," Belinda said, trying to be cheery. "Isn't this a Norman Rockwell painting?"

"More like Norman Bates," was all Rachel could say as she turned to take the journey up the creaky stairs to check out the bedrooms.

The fly's name was Roxanne, and she was one of Willy's best scouts. She was fast and smart and knew all the tricks when it came to surveillance. She also had no fear of the humans, a rare trait in a world filled with flypaper traps and toxic sprays that stopped bugs dead.

"Here's the lowdown," Roxanne reported to Willy. "Boy. Girl. Mommy. And The Woman. She's got to have the biggest forehead I've ever seen. It's like a smooth, shiny boulder up there."

"Roxanne . . ." Willy was trying to be patient.

"Okay, okay. From the looks of the place, I'd say you've got a better chance of growing a stinger on your butt than anyone moving into that mess. And the place is a wreck, Willy."

Willy continued his flight toward the house, just ahead of hundreds of his young insect followers. "Hey, a little dirt never killed anyone. They'll move in. I know it."

Roxanne kept her pace with Willy and looked him in the eye. "Give it up, Willy. Nobody human is ever gonna live in that stink hole. The Alliance has made sure of it."

And even though what Roxanne said was true, and the Elders and their constant raids on the property *had* ruined what was rumored to have been a glorious house, Willy wouldn't give up. He needed to see these people for himself—needed to find out if they might be the ones to bring human life back to the Pond. Unlike the Elders, he was convinced humans were part of the balance that would keep the Pond healthy and alive. And if these people were the ones, it was his job to make sure the Alliance didn't chase them away.

High above the property, the crows began their descent just as Rachel pried open the tiny window in a bedroom she imagined would be hers. It was one of two smaller rooms that she was sure would put her farthest from where her mother would be. It also overlooked the water, which Rachel swore she couldn't care less about. But looking out, even cynical Rachel had to admit that the view of pond and trees was pretty nice, especially compared to the brick-wall vista of her room back in the city.

The first crow smashed through the screen, which of course was broken anyway. Rachel screamed. Then she screamed again as three more fierce dark birds flew into the room.

Downstairs, Belinda reacted by timidly suggesting that Rachel must be very excited by the second-floor view. But when they all watched a shrieking Rachel bolt down the stairs, followed by several birds, it was clear the outdoor sights had nothing to do with her excitement.

Rachel opened the door and rushed outside, giving the remainder of the squadron entrance to the house. As planned, the birds aimed directly for the humans.

Slouched down in his chair, Oliver was amazed at the crows' accuracy. He watched two of them chase Belinda around the living room. It was like a cartoon.

"This is so great!" Oliver said aloud, as the crows flew and dove and called out their sick twisted laughs. He was actually enjoying this so much that, for the first time in hours, Oliver turned off the Game Boy.

The General looked on with pride as his squadron of fighters showed they had learned their lessons well. Fast, swooping moves that made the humans dance and scream. Snapping beaks that threatened pain. Loud screeching "*caaaawwwwws*" that were meant to strike fear in their hearts. It was all perfect. Even Antoine seemed on mark—aiming to attack the small boy who was alone near the fireplace.

"Steady. Eyes straight. Beak firm," Antoine urged himself. "This will show them. I'm no loser!"

The crow focused, picked up speed, and—*smoosh!*—made immediate contact—with the chair.

Antoine was mortified. How the heck could he have missed? What was his problem? Yanking his beak out of the cushion, Antoine turned to attack again. But the boy wasn't moving. Antoine was beak to nose with this smiling human, and the kid wasn't scared—not even a little!

Imagining the belittling voice of his uncle in his head, Antoine snapped back to his mission. He narrowed his gaze and did the only thing he could think of. He bit the boy's nose.

Willy heard two distinct screams: first came Rachel's, who thought she'd escaped the birds by running toward the safety of the Pond only to be pecked at by the two Black Angel crows who'd been hiding in a pine tree.

The second was Oliver's. The shriek that escaped his lungs scared even him.

Willy halted his insects. He knew what was happening. "The Elders are trying to chase them away! We must take action. Don't let the humans leave!"

Immediately, swarms of flying bugs gathered in a cloud and flew off toward the house.

"Do your best! It's up to us!" called the young dragonfly to his kin.

Mooch finally caught up with his friend. He was out of breath from trying to keep the pace . . . and so what if he'd stopped for a quick beetle or two.

"Willy, send me. Let me help." Mooch was panting and exhausted but wanted desperately to be included.

But Willy couldn't hear anything except the inner voice that urged him on. It was a voice he'd later regret listening to—the same voice that somehow gave him the power to turn to his friend and say, "Get lost, Mooch! You don't belong!"

And then he flew off, leaving Mooch all alone once again. His first impulse was to agree with Willy. He didn't belong and should just leave. But that reaction gave way to anger and defiance.

"I'll show you, Willy," he said aloud as he followed behind the swarming, crawling buzz of insect attackers. "I do belong, Willy. I do."

Inside the house, Oliver's mom was tending to his nose. "You'll be fine, honey," she said as she applied a swab of antibacterial-soaked cotton. She was one of those mothers whose purse resembled a drugstore. Disinfectant wipes. Band-Aids. Finger splints. For once, Oliver was glad to have a mother who was always prepared for the worst.

Ten feet away, Antoine hid behind a wood beam up in the corner of the ceiling. He should've been basking in a glow of pride and strength, but instead he felt embarrassed and even ashamed that he had hurt the boy.

He smacked his head against the ceiling. "Lo-ser! I am *such* a loser," he muttered to himself.

Suddenly, a raw loud cackle cut through the room, freezing everyone in place. The General burst through the screened-in porch and flew directly at Oliver and his mother. Antoine cowered as he watched it all unfold in slow motion. The General closed in on his target, with claws extended like knives.

Antoine couldn't quite explain what happened next. Later, under questioning, he had no answer for why he did what he did. But in that very instant, before The General could strike, Antoine swooped down and knocked his own flesh and blood off course and onto the floor.

Stunned, both nephew and uncle lay on the ground near the fireplace hearth. The noise of their crash startled Oliver and his mother enough to get themselves up and into the safety of the kitchen, where Belinda Shrank was pretending to examine the fine craftsmanship inside the broom closet.

Antoine could practically hear the blood boiling inside his uncle. "You . . . you . . ." The General rose up, towering over the little crow.

"I know." Antoine cringed. "Iiiidiot."

Outside, Rachel was defending herself with an old garbage can lid. As the crows continued to dive-bomb for her head, she deflected their attacks with the makeshift shield.

"Don't mess with me, birds!" she shouted as they bounced off the lid, beaks bent in pain. "I'm from the city!"

Suddenly, a cloud of mosquitoes, flies, bees, and wasps appeared. How could Rachel have known that they were on her side? What person would ever think insects could be allies and not stinging, buzzing foes?

It was a dark mass—and it was closing in on *her*.

Mooch popped out of the thicket of cattails just in time to hear the girl's deafening shriek. He turned toward the loud noise and watched her snap into action. She became a machine of swinging arms and swatting hands, and the poor insects knew only that now they had to defend themselves from this madwoman while getting her away from another crow assault. The insect swarm encased her, descended on her like an alien spaceship, hoping they could then lead her back into the house. But it was all too much for her. Rachel held the garbage lid over her head and started crying hysterically.

Oliver came running out of the house, followed by his mother, who managed to carry Rachel back inside.

The insects were thrilled to see the girl disappear behind the front door, and they erupted in high-pitched cheers and wing-to-wing slaps that marked a job well done.

Oliver just stood there. He watched as the insect swarm flew off toward the few remaining crows, who were still a bit dizzy from coming in contact with Rachel's garbage can lid. It looked like the insects were actually chasing the birds away, or so Oliver thought. Weird.

He turned to head back inside, but then his eye caught

the spotted tail of a small creature disappearing between the tall grass by the pond. Curious, Oliver walked over to explore.

Mooch had stopped beside the water. His feet ached and his mouth was dry and his belly rumbled with the need for food. He dipped his mouth into the Pond to take a sip, to cool his toes, to hunt for bugs.

And that's when his life changed. Because when he looked up, there was a boy, stretching out his hand. It was just like what the human children did in the Forbidden Zone when they would offer him yummy candy or bite-sized pieces of their lunch. Mooch knew an open hand always meant good things to eat, so he took the offer seriously, walking two or three steps closer to the boy.

Oliver couldn't believe that the funny-looking lizard was actually coming to him. He'd had only one pet before, a goldfish, that lasted a whole week before going belly-up in the fish tank that he now used for his flies. It might be kind of cool to take this guy home and watch him hunt the bugs like some sort of insect safari.

"Here you go. . . . Just a little more . . ."

Mooch took tentative steps and was instantly disappointed when he saw that the boy's hand was empty. But Oliver was thrilled. "I caught a lizard! Mom, I caught a lizard," he yelled, scooping up the clammy creature.

Mooch was in shock. And his feelings were hurt again. "I'm not a lizard," he moaned. "I'm a salamander, stupid!"

Back inside the house, Oliver's mom had chased the last crow away with a broom. The strange onslaught of birds and bugs appeared to be over. Rachel was behind the ratty couch, scratching at the road map of bug bites on her arms and legs, and Oliver walked in holding a squirmy something in his cupped hands.

Belinda emerged from her hiding spot in the kitchen, thankful she'd taken the unusual step of having Carol sign a personal-injury release form before showing her the property. "You know what, y'all?" she said in as folksy a tone as she could muster. "There's a lovely two-bedroom apartment near the Kentucky Fried Chicken, and . . ."

But Carol cut her off with the three loveliest words Belinda had ever heard.

"We'll take it."

CHAPTER EIGHT

THE NEWS of Mooch's capture spread around the Pond like a crackling bolt of summer lightning. It had been a week since that fateful day, and the abduction was still on everyone's mind.

The Alliance Elders, of course, used it as another example of just how horrible humans were. Frankie, the frog, was so outraged, he gathered the amphibians in a twenty-one tongue salute to the missing Mooch.

"I told you all before," moaned Flakes, scratching his turtle shell against the jagged rock behind him, "dis is da beginning of da end."

53

The turtle wasn't just always itchy, he was also always certain that the demise of the Pond was just a deer dropping away. "I'm just thankful we gots each other," he said. "Strength in numbers, right?"

The others had to agree. By creating an alliance, they had made life by the Pond peaceful and safe after the destruction brought about so many years ago, when the only rules they lived by were dictated by the food chain, the weather, and the man who had come to destroy it all.

His name was Byron Trumble, a rich man with a fat life, thanks to the paper mill he'd built just ten miles from Little Falls. Back then the townspeople he employed were grateful for the jobs he gave them, turning hundred-year-old trees into reams of newsprint, stationery, and toilet paper.

"What's good for PulpPaper is good for Little Falls," was the slogan that seemed to be everywhere from bumper stickers to billboards. Unfortunately, what was good for the town wasn't quite as good for the streams and rivers that the factory's waste spilled into.

The Pond fell victim, changing colors every week, depending on the color of paper being made. Blues, greens, yellows, all flowed downstream and mixed into a stinky palette of pond scum. To make matters worse, the toxic runoff killed the fish and any other wild thing that it came in contact with—all in the name of a softer, more absorbent tissue.

The Pond turned into a gross, uninhabitable stink hole. None of the animals knew what was causing the mess, just that it was devastating. To the Pond creatures it was an anonymous crime. An unsolved mystery.

All that changed the day bulldozers tore down a high-rise squirrel apartment, destroying the tree like the snap of a toothpick. Byron Trumble had seen the Pond from an airplane and wanted to own it the same way he owned everything, down to the politicians who looked the other way no matter what laws he broke.

He was the one who carved out the bumpy road, cleared hundreds of trees (which he conveniently turned into wallpaper), and built the little house.

Initially, the Pond's inhabitants were curious about the skinny man stomping around the woods in his bright white shoes. But their curiosity turned to fear after the first shotgun spree mowed down foxes, then pheasants, and then anything that moved or flew nearby.

The different species were no longer each other's greatest enemies. The awful man in the bright white shoes held that honor. It was now up to the six families to find a way to make their lives safe again. By forming allies, they were creating strength, which became the sole purpose of The Alliance.

Sitting alone in their hiding spot under the maple tree, Willy couldn't stop blaming himself for Mooch's capture.

"If I hadn't made up with him, and if I hadn't included him in my stupid secrets . . ." But what was done was done. Mooch was gone, and Willy was stuck inside a cocoon of guilt.

Willy kept going over the final events of that day. First came the news from Roxanne that Mooch was caught. And then after he'd called off the insect march, Willy remembered flying as fast as he could to the house, arriving just in time to see the people loading into a van, Mooch grasped in the boy's pudgy hands.

Willy's heart sank. He knew it was all his fault. But his self-directed anger changed to excitement the moment he saw the lady take down the FOR SALE sign. The people were buying the house! They would move in!

He flew through the air and zigzagged to the window of the van. He tried to get Mooch's attention by banging his wings against the glass.

But Willy could tell that Mooch was in no mood for celebration. He looked scared and confused.

The truth was that Mooch also blamed Willy for his troubles. So when he looked up and saw his dragonfly *ex*-friend fluttering outside the window, he turned away.

Rachel had a different reaction. Seeing the dragonfly banging against the window, she burst into tears and hid under an old blanket in the backseat of the van, mumbling in a language that only Belinda Shrank fully understood.

* * *

"Your new house is just three hours from the city," said Arthur Durkin cheerfully. "We can get together on weekends. Go hiking or canoeing! And if I'm not mistaken," he continued, "BioProsthesis just opened a new research lab near there. I bet I'll be up all the time."

It was a lie both Rachel and Oliver knew well. Their father was always painting himself as an active, outdoorsy guy, but the truth was he worked almost every weekend and broke out in hives if he so much as looked at a tree. Besides that, thanks to countless missed birthday parties and forgotten school plays, they'd both come to know he was a great promiser, and a lousy doer.

Arthur had stopped by the apartment to get a few remaining things, and to say good-bye to the kids. Standing among the stacked cardboard boxes, Oliver couldn't help but think how squirmy his father looked as he watched the life he no longer had get sealed up tight.

Packing up his own room was a piece of cake for Oliver. He simply took two empty boxes and threw in everything that would fit. Clothes, toys, books—they all got crammed in together. Then, before his mother could inspect what he'd done, he taped the boxes closed and marked each one: MINE.

Rachel, on the other hand, hadn't packed a single thing. Oliver kept reminding her that the movers would be there in the morning, but she just sat on her bed, staring at the ceiling, trying desperately to think of a way *not* to move to Little Falls. "I could run away. To Paris. Or Switzerland. They make really good chocolate."

"I dunno. Zits and calories—they'll both eventually get ya." Cherise was over to help, which only made the reality of what was happening more awful.

"I'm moving. I'm really, truly moving."

Watching his sister and her best friend go through the pain of saying good-bye, Oliver was actually relieved he didn't have any friends that mattered like that. Or at least that's what he told himself.

"I am going to miss you, like, *so-o-o* much." Cherise was crying, which made Rachel start to cry, which made Oliver think once again that girls are so weird.

Mooch had never been more frightened in his whole life. He was stuck in a glass cage, a prisoner of the hideous boy. Thankfully, the kid had the good sense to feed him the fresh flies he caught regularly. But why did he have to pull off the crunchy wings, and why did he seem to enjoy mutilating insects so much?

"Who do we have here?" Oliver's dad was on his knees, his face pressed close to the glass. Mooch peered back, and could see right up this man's nose—a sight more frightening than anything he'd ever seen at the Pond.

"He's my new pet. My lizard."

Arthur smiled. "He's not a lizard, Ollie. He's a salamander. An amphibian. Life expectancy: ten to twelve years. Diet: insects, worms, and larvae."

Wow, thought Mooch with a grin. This guy's a fan.

Even Oliver was impressed that his father knew so much about something that interested him. His dad usually just went on and on about polymer plastics and kinetics and other junk that made Oliver's mind go numb.

"Mind if I get a closer look?" asked Arthur, whose arm was already reaching into the cage.

Mooch's sense of security suddenly wilted. He cowered into a corner as the large hand crept closer. Oh man, I'm dead, he thought, suddenly hearing the voice of his mother, who was perpetually warning him how dreadful humans were.

Arthur cupped his fingers under Mooch and lifted him out of the cage. He examined him with an expert eye, tracing his fingers along Mooch's tail, tickling the moist skin with his fingernail. "Did you know that if you cut their tails off, they'll grow back?"

Even though he knew it was true, hearing that made Mooch practically pass out. But Oliver's eyes widened with a sudden interest. "No way! That's impossible."

"No. It's one of those great tricks that exists only in nature. For now, anyway." Arthur looked straight into Mooch's frightened eyes and poked his soft underbelly with his thumb. "Tell you what, sport. Let's get a knife and test the theory. See if this tail grows back or not."

"What?" Oliver grabbed Mooch from his father and

put him back into the tank. "He's not an experiment. He's my friend."

Oliver looked at his father with a scowl. Once again, just as he was feeling closer, his dad had said something that exploded the bridge between them. And, as always, instead of trying to fix the mistake, his dad continued to make it worse. "You can't be friends with a salamander, son. Grow up."

Oliver couldn't wait to move.

"I ain't gonna sit on my big butt and wait for disaster. It's not my style." A rumor had been circulating, and Pudge was outraged at the suggestion that the Alliance was not going to react decisively to these recent events. "We must meet the situation head-on. Fight first—ask questions later."

The Insects, Reptiles, Mammals, and Birds responded with cheers. The General smiled with evil glee. But the Amphibians were less enthusiastic. This latest problem may or may not have been related to Mooch's capture, and they wanted to take a cautious approach to the situation.

"I dunno," croaked Frankie, who was distracted by the erratic flight pattern of a firefly. "I suggest more of a 'wait and see' approach. In fact . . ."

Splat! Out went his sticky tongue, aimed for the firefly. Unfortunately, he was off-target as usual, which Frankie realized the instant the sharp burrs of a burdock bush disappeared into his slobbering mouth.

Nobody dared laugh as the mammoth frog first gagged and then struggled to swallow. Frankie had no choice but to pull his big round eyes down through his head and use them to help push the thorny plant down his throat.

"Ahhhh, now where was I? Oh yeah, *urrrp!*" The frog's digestive eruption was heard clear across the Pond.

The meeting went on like that most of the night. Some points got argued, some decisions got made, but mostly the Alliance was once again caught in the struggle of trying to connect every mishap around the Pond to the humans.

"The fish say it is certain now. The humans will ruin us," the beaver said, translating the concerns of the trout Elders.

Fat Mama raised up on her legs. "Ask them if they've got any real reason to worry. Any evidence?"

The beaver nodded, then slipped off to the water's edge. Air bubbles rose and popped up on the surface as he spoke to the uneasy fish. A minute later, he raised his dripping head out of the water, then turned to address the Alliance.

"Just as you feared," the beaver began. "Twelve dead fish. Reasons unknown."

The next day was a blur for Oliver and his family. The movers arrived an hour late, broke Carol's favorite lamp, and nearly dropped the couch down three flights of narrow stairs.

Oliver made sure that no one touched his salamander tank. Even though it was heavy, he managed to carry it by himself. By two o'clock the apartment was packed up and the truck was ready to roll. Rachel sobbed in the front seat of the car, and Oliver sat in the back with Mooch's tank safely strapped in next to him.

The ride took forever and Mooch had no idea what was going on. He felt every bump in the road and slid across his tank every time the car made a turn. The boy kept a close eye on him, though, and even smiled a few times, which Mooch had to admit took away some of the anxiety. But the longer he stayed inside that car, the more worried he became that he'd never smell fresh air again.

He eventually accepted that he was off on an adventure. Maybe this was his chance to finally see new sights. New creatures. New snacks.

But when the car finally stopped, he was shocked to see he was right back where he had started.

At the ugly house by the Pond.

CHAPTER NINE

OLIVER WAS LOSING his mind. He'd been alone in the house for exactly two hours and twenty-three minutes, and the only thing he'd been able to get on TV was the educational channel. And that was only after carefully balancing a fork on a twisted clothes hanger and connecting them both to the television with paper clips.

After a seemingly never-ending week of frantic unpacking, it was Saturday again, and he finally had the whole house to himself for the afternoon. Rachel had gotten scammed into helping their mom set up her science room at the high school, which Oliver thought was absolutely nuts. Oliver felt that setting foot in a school before the end of summer vacation was against all known rules of childhood. School was a full week away, and nothing short of free cable would get him even near the place. And now, with a full day ahead and absolutely nothing to do, the reality of life without good reception was setting in.

Oliver turned to the glass tank by the window. "You have no idea what I'd give for a satellite dish right about now, lizard."

Mooch cringed. His name had been reduced to this slur since being caught by the kid a few weeks ago. And though hearing it still made his cold blood boil, he resigned himself to the fact that the kid was stupid and he'd better just get used to it.

Getting used to things seemed to be a way of life for Mooch now. He was almost starting to feel comfortable in his small, glass-walled prison. Sure he was lonely for his friends, the few that he had not eaten. And the freedom to run and play outside—that was long gone. But as far as his stomach was concerned, this "being fed" thing was pretty darn good. All he had to do was bang his tiny hand on the glass, get the boy's attention, and the kid just *gave* him food! It was amazingly simple. Freshly caught flies. Beetles. Even a piece of this thing the kid himself was eating—something called "cheeseburger." Mooch had no idea what it was, but wow, did he like it.

After three weeks Mooch had the kid pretty well trained, at least for the feeding part. He wasn't so quick on the cleanup duty or fresh water thing, but these were small drawbacks Mooch was willing to deal with. As long as he was fed, he was one happy salamander.

It was a sparkling late summer day. The few clouds above drifted slowly across the sky as if they were floating on their backs, lazily enjoying the afternoon. It was perfect weather for a hike or a swim or just to read a book underneath the shade of a tree, which of course explained why Oliver was inside fretting over how to watch his television.

Wandering from room to room looking for inspiration, Oliver was desperate. He knew he wanted to make some sort of antenna, but wasn't finding anything he could use. He briefly considered snapping off the long extendable aerial attached to Rachel's boom box, but the thought of her wrath drove him back to his senses.

Guzzling a can of grape soda, he looked out the window in the back of the house, and that's when the idea hit. There was an old shed out there that was in such bad shape it made the lopsided house look like a million-dollar chateau. Rachel, of course, refused to even look at the thing, but Oliver had explored the cramped dusty place when they first arrived, braving the cobwebs and smell of rotting wood and animal decay.

He remembered that, among the rusted old tools and

broken furniture, was a bent metal aerial antenna, like the kind he'd seen on some rooftops in the city. In the past he'd always pitied the poor losers who had to grab their images from the airwaves instead of having the convenience of clearly delivered satellite or fiber-optic cable; but now he was one of those losers.

Oliver knew two things: 1. He had to get on the roof. And 2. His mother would freak if she knew he had gone up there. Weighing his options, he decided he'd take his chances with the mother thing, since getting more than one channel was worth almost any punishment he could imagine.

He rummaged through the shed and uncovered the ancient antenna, then carried it to the side of the yard. Next, he propped a creaky wooden ladder against the house. It was nearly long enough to reach the roof—but was still short by about a foot. He decided to climb as far as he could and deal with the problem once he got there.

"Channel heaven, here I come!" Oliver said triumphantly as he tied one end of a long frayed rope to the old antenna.

Clutching the end of the rope, he began his climb. As the ladder groaned, he could tell that it probably wasn't safe; but he was so determined, he just kept going. One foot. Then the next. Higher. And higher.

When he got to the top rung he turned to look back down. Big mistake. The distance between him and the ground made him dizzy just at the moment that his weight began to crack the top rung of the ladder.

The sound of breaking wood froze him in place. If the fall didn't kill him, he knew his mother would—an image that propelled him to hoist himself up onto the roof using all the strength his arms could give.

Unfortunately in his haste to save his butt, he kicked the ladder, which swung away from the house and toppled into his mother's newly planted flower bed.

"I'm dead," he moaned. He was now stuck there, a fact that may have deterred an ordinary kid. But Oliver was determined. He would set up the antenna and deal with getting down later.

Antoine was still in big trouble with The General. Ever since the fiasco at the house, when he'd interfered with the attack on the human mother and son, he'd been kicked out of the squadron and now spent his days scavenging for food with the lowlifes on the garbage crew.

These crows were the dregs of the species and were all former thieves and delinquents, crows who'd flown on the wrong side of the Pond. Their rogue days behind them, the garbage crew now combed the mounds of trash for buried treasures. It was also these crows' job to keep unwanted visitors from any of the good stuff: rotted animal carcasses, half-full pizza boxes, the occasional tossed out compost heap. It was dirty work, and the stink took some getting used to. But the General thought a little tough love might straighten his nephew out . . . and give himself some space from the embarrassment of that day.

The garbage dump lay just a mile or so from the Pond, its ugliness hidden from the road by a row of pine trees. Though an eyesore to the humans, the mountains of discarded trash and bent and broken things was a site of natural beauty to the scavengers who called it home.

Rats. Maggots and flies. The occasional raccoon. All were drawn by the lovely filth and rotting stench. For those with the proper palette, it was a popular fast-food destination that served up something new every day.

As scary as it was at first, Antoine actually loved his new assignment. He didn't have to pretend to be someone he wasn't, and was surprised that no one made fun of him here; they just accepted him as the screwup he was. The weird part, though—now that he wasn't under the watchful eye of his intense uncle—he *wasn't* a screwup. Well, not as much of one, anyway.

Man, thought Antoine as he dug into a pile of stinky old fruit and coffee grounds. This is the life!

Mooch had no idea where the kid had gone. All he knew was he was hungry. He banged on the glass and tossed clawfuls of gravel—but no one came. He plopped back down on his tummy and waited, listening to a steady thumping sound that seemed to be coming from on top of the roof.

Oliver had never been so intent on accomplishing a task. Nothing was going to stop him as he worked under the hot sun with one thing on his mind: The Simpsons at four o'clock.

The antenna proved to be in pretty good shape, and he banged it into the sloped shingled roof with as many nails as he could, hooking them against the metal in hopes that it would hold.

"Man, it is so hot up here," he said, taking a short break to wipe the sweat from his face. He sat on the roof for a moment and looked out at the view.

From the height of the roof, Oliver could see the shape and scope of the pond from an entirely new perspective. He'd never really noticed the many intricate little inlets that disappeared into the tall weeds, or the low log that jutted out of the water ten or twenty yards from the far shore. Beyond the water he now saw a set of small rocky cliffs, and thought that if he were a different kind of kid, he'd want to go explore them. But he was not that kid. He was a TV kid, and the truth was, he couldn't wait to get back inside.

With the antenna firmly in place, Oliver unspooled the metal coil he'd carried up in his knapsack and dangled the loose end down until it reached the sill of his open window. He'd taken down his mother's clothesline—the one she'd fashioned out of a long piece of wire—and the wet clothes she'd just washed were scattered on the grass below. He'd get into big trouble for that too, but he figured, once you step in a pile of trouble—your shoes are already covered in it.

High above him a pair of blue jays flew across the sky. He wouldn't have even noticed except for the sudden splat of bird poop that narrowly missed him. It made him feel like he'd been a target. The thought made him laugh, imagining a couple of birds actually aiming for him. What a goof!

The two blue jays, Max and Doris, were disappointed they'd missed. "I told you the wind would take it left," argued Max.

"Excuse me, Mr. I-can't-be-wrong. You said *right*," Doris shot back.

"No, featherbrain—I said *left!*"

"Well, I distinctly heard RIGHT!"

"Then you distinctly heard WRONG!"

Anyone who knew them, knew this was normal. Max and Doris never agreed except to disagree, and since between them they only had about half a brain, it didn't take much to get either of them confused.

The argument continued as the couple flew haphazardly away, just narrowly missing General Santo Domingo, who was on a solo patrol of the area.

"Birdbrains!" yelled The General as he swerved up at the last second to avoid smacking into the arguing blue jays.

And had it not been for that near collision, The

General would never have seen the thing that lifted his heart. For as he broke from his flight pattern, he noticed that on the roof below was the boy he'd wanted to attack. And now he had the chance to teach that kid—and his nephew—a lesson they'd both never forget.

"You're somethin' else, you know that, Antoine?" Reggie, a bent-beaked garbage crow, was lying next to a worn-out tire, eating something that once might've been a melon. His head rested on his scarred wing, injured years ago in a fight with a deranged duck. "I mean, you could use a little meat on them skinny bones, but I like you. You're O-kay."

Antoine grinned. No crow had ever said anything nice to him. So what if Reggie was a crook, a liar, and a cheat. He thought Antoine was "O-kay." And by default, that made Reggie the best friend he'd ever had.

"Ten-hut!" The sudden shout shocked Antoine back to reality. The General was standing in front of him, looking down with scornful eyes.

"Who's the stiff?" asked Reggie as he spat out a seed that landed by The General's left claw.

But Antoine didn't even have time to answer before his uncle yanked him up to his feet and told him to stay in formation. They flew off without another word.

Oliver knew nothing about how television signals worked, or how this antenna would turn them into his favorite shows. He only knew he was almost done. He was just fastening the long wire to the antenna when he heard the noise.

"*Caw! Caw! Caaaaaw!*"

He assumed it was just another bird, maybe the same ones who'd tried to poop on him. He didn't look up—just kept working. He was so close!

"Watch closely. Chances like this don't happen every day, Antoine," his uncle said, directing Antoine's attention to the roof. "You can wipe the slate clean, boy. Go right to the head of the class."

Antoine didn't want to have anything to do with his uncle's revenge. He didn't want to attack the boy. He didn't even want to be reinstated as a Black Angel. But when The General gives an order, it's pretty tough to say no, especially when he's so mad at you. So Antoine took a deep breath, closed his eyes, and dove straight for the boy.

The General smiled. He knew his nephew would most likely miss, which was why he planned to go in for the second pass and make the boy bleed.

Oliver put the last tight twist on the screw. "I did it! Channel seven—here I come."

Triumphantly, he turned, and was shocked to see the black shape swooping down from the sky, getting closer and closer. For once, Antoine was dead-on.

"*Cawwww!*" Antoine called out, more as a warning than anything else.

Oliver didn't have to time to think—just react. He jumped to his feet and started to run along the shabby roof. And to Antoine's own (and The General's) amazement, the young crow followed right behind the boy.

Oliver had a big problem on his hands. He knew the bird was getting closer, but so was the end of the roof. The image of his mother coming home to find her flower bed ruined, the clothes all over the lawn, and her only son sprawled on the ground made him stop.

For his part, Antoine kept on his mark. Impact should be in five . . . four . . . three . . . two . . .

Down in Oliver's room, Mooch heard a thundering crash that shook his tank, spilling the water in his tiny dish.

Twelve feet above him, just as Antoine's speeding beak made contact with Oliver's chest, the roof caved in. Both crow and boy came crashing down into a cramped attic thick with dust and ancient mice droppings.

Oliver knew he was in huge trouble. But Antoine just felt lucky. Fate had intervened, and he didn't have to hurt the boy. High above them both, The General flew off in disgust. Antoine had messed up again.

Antoine shook himself to make sure he was A-OK. First came the relief that all his body parts seemed to be attached, but he was a bit shocked that his left wing appeared to be bent feebly in a right angle by his side.

"That can't be good," the crow said to himself.

Oliver carefully wiggled each leg, making sure they still worked. Everything seemed okay. But why did his back hurt so much? Oliver moaned. He was sure that he'd broken his spine! Images of spending his life in a wheelchair, being fed through some automated tube thing, flashed through his mind. And for what? A stupid television! He swore he'd never watch the dumb thing again. Ever!

Oliver took a deep breath, then reached behind his back, searching for a puddle of blood, a broken bone, or some other evidence of a horrendous injury. Instead, his hand grasped something smooth, angular, and somehow wonderful.

"Look what we found," Oliver said to the injured crow by his side.

Antoine watched as Oliver slowly opened his fingers. They both gasped softly as a faint golden light glowed from a large gem in his hand.

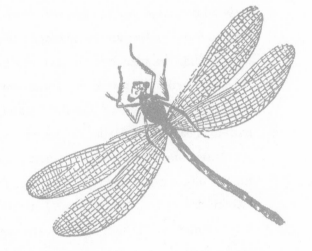

CHAPTER TEN

EY, THIS PLACE ain't so bad."

Antoine was relaxing inside the birdcage Oliver had found in the decrepit shed. His wing was set in a splint, and he knew it would be weeks before he'd fly again, which was just fine with him. Considering how badly the attack on Oliver had gone, he was happy to be safely behind bars, and not outside facing his uncle's steely-eyed anger.

"Say, whatcha thinking over there?" Antoine called over to Mooch, trying to break the ice with the quiet salamander.

Mooch had been thrilled to have a new roommate—for about an hour. That was how long it took to realize that the crow, whose name was Antoine, was a constant yakker who seemed to enjoy the sound of his own raw voice as much as Mooch liked the silence of his daydreams.

"I've seen you around the Pond. You hang with that dragonfly kid, don'tcha?" Antoine rattled the metal cage with his beak. "Huh? Hello? I'm talking over here."

"I used to," replied Mooch quietly, as he chomped on the last bits of worm that Oliver had scrounged up for him. "We kinda went our separate ways."

"Ooh, gossip. Details, please." Antoine was now pressing his beak through the bars of the cage in anticipation of a good juicy story. But Mooch chose to stay silent, and turned away to stare out the window at the blue cloudless sky instead.

As much as he was dying to, Oliver hadn't had much time to examine the strange gem he'd found. Between replanting the flowers he'd ruined, helping Belinda Shrank's husband, Freddy, repair the huge hole in the roof, and apologizing to his mother for pretty much *everything*—he was one busy kid.

His mom was still seething. She wished she could've grounded him, but Oliver had no social life, so it was a punishment without consequences. Oliver knew a better sentence would be to *un*-ground him and force him to go out and make friends. But they all knew the truth;

where would a kid like him make friends in a place like this?

Instead, his mother had him try and fix all the things he'd messed up. And she'd taken away the TV for a month.

There were two positive things that came out of the whole "roof incident" (as it was called around the house). First, they all now knew that there was a small attic above the second floor. It wasn't tall enough for standing, but Oliver's mother figured that once they cleaned it and patched all the leaks, she'd have some extra storage.

The second good thing: Oliver was allowed to keep the disabled crow until his wing healed properly. Even though the crazy bird had tried to attack him, it was because of that weird accident that Oliver now had the gemstone; so he figured caring for the crow was the least he could do to repay the bird for its role in the discovery.

Sweating in the garden, working off his punishment, Oliver hated that Rachel was actually happy that he was in so much trouble. "Takes the spotlight off of me," she slyly told him from the comfort of a lounge chair.

Oliver was dying to tell Rachel what had really happened. How the crow had attacked him and how he had found the cool shiny gem. But he knew the bird part would freak her out, and the strange jewel thing was his personal find. She had a big mouth when it came to private stuff like that.

So it was a delicious golden secret that was now

hidden beneath the socks in his dresser drawer; a secret that only he and that weird little crow knew about.

Oliver's final week of vacation evaporated right before his eyes. He didn't get to do half the things he wanted before summer ended, but even he knew it was his own fault. The night before school, his dreams were filled with anonymous faces speaking strange languages that he couldn't understand. When his mother finally roused him, reality struck him hard and fast. School was waiting. Unlike his sister, who was consumed with fear and anxiety about starting her new life in a new school, he wasn't worried. Oliver accepted that he was an unknown entity in an alien environment. He only hoped he could be as invisible as possible.

"Kids, hurry up! It's my first day too!" Downstairs, Oliver's mother was running around, trying to stay calm and failing miserably.

Both Mooch and Antoine could tell that something was different. The boy always slept late and woke up when he wanted to. But today the kid was up at the crack of dawn and making a ton of noise as he dressed. How annoying.

"Tell the kid to keep it down," Antoine moaned, trying to get at least another hour of shut-eye.

Mooch really didn't care that the boy was up. As long as the kid fed him, anyway. But Oliver was too rushed to remember feeding anyone but himself, and quickly bolted out of his room and raced downstairs for breakfast.

"Great. No food," said a grumpy, hungry Mooch. Hopeless, he collapsed onto his belly and did everything he could to NOT think about food, which, of course just made visions of tasty treats dance in his head.

The sound of racing footsteps on stairs snapped Mooch's attention back to the here and now. Of course the kid had remembered! Three cheers for food! The door burst open and Oliver looked at his two pets briefly before turning to his dresser. He rummaged through the top drawer as the car horn honked fiercely outside.

"I'm coming! Hold your horses!" he yelled as socks and underwear went flying everywhere. Suddenly he stopped, and his hand pulled out the shiny golden gem. "For good luck," he said out loud before jamming it deep into his jeans pocket. He was out the door in seconds, leaving a starving salamander and curious crow behind.

"Them's the breaks, huh, pal?" said Antoine, hoping to kick-start a conversation with Mooch.

But Mooch just slowly turned his head toward Antoine. He narrowed his eyes and chose his words carefully. "Shut your fat beak already!" The crow was shocked. Frankly, so was Mooch. But the rest of the day was spent in glorious silence.

"Okay. Here's the deal," began Rachel, addressing Oliver and his mother as they drove to their new first day of school. "No one says hello to me or acknowledges in any way that we're related. Deal?"

This was the first time Oliver and Rachel had been in the same school building since grade school. And now, Rachel was feeling the added pressure of having their mother there too.

The car pulled to a stop in the parking lot, and there it was—the new school. Unlike their schools in the city, the large brick building was surrounded by grass and manicured playing fields instead of chipped concrete and chain-link fences.

Rachel walked away from the car quickly, hoping no one had seen her emerge from the teacher's lot. Oliver followed a few moments behind, and for once felt confident that everything was going to be okay.

It was a feeling that didn't last long.

The very moment he stepped inside his classroom, every eyeball was on him. The hushed murmur of "new kid" spread around the room, and like a hot branding iron on his butt, he was indelibly labeled.

The history teacher, a tall stoop-shouldered man named Mr. Bertram, looked Oliver up and down as if trying to guess his weight, and then pointed to an empty seat near the back. Oliver walked what felt like three miles to his desk. His new sneakers squeaked on the varnished floor. His pants legs rubbed together, making what seemed to him a deafening *whoosh-whoosh* sound with every step.

To make matters worse, he sneezed, loud and wet, all over the girl in front of him.

Oliver was anything but invisible.

The day crawled forward like a slug—leaving a slimy sticky trail behind it. Oliver felt smaller and smaller with every hour. Kids can be really mean, and Oliver had always been way at the bottom of the school food chain. He was an easy mark for anyone wanting to feel better about him or herself, a trait that unfortunately followed him to the new school.

At 10:15, Bradley Humphrey tripped Oliver in the hallway, spilling boy and books—much to everyone's delight. At 12:22, a girl—whose nickname was Nibbles—dropped a glob of green Jell-O on his lunchroom chair just before he sat down. And at 1:33, two older boys cornered him in the boys' room and demanded he pay them a dollar.

More humiliated than scared, Oliver reached into his pants pocket, looking for some change to give them. That's when he felt the smooth gem. He'd totally forgotten he'd brought it. Some good-luck charm, he thought, before confessing he had no money. The thugs let Oliver go—only after extracting a promise that he pay them double the next day.

And that is why Oliver sat in his last class of his first day, hating everything. How was he going to survive the week, let alone the school year?

In the front of the classroom, the teacher droned on

and on about geometric shapes, but Oliver didn't even try to listen. Instead he was busy watching the minute hand of the clock inch slowly toward his freedom.

Absently, Oliver slid his hand inside his pocket and slipped out the gemstone. Warm and golden, it was amazing to hold, and as he stared into it, he could see veins stretching through the glassy thickness. He felt like he could make out the abstract designs of some ancient artwork. Or a twisted map. Or anything that wasn't the reality of his miserable life.

The slow buzzing sound of a fly caught his attention. Narrowing his gaze, Oliver watched the fly dart near him. It landed for a split second on the red ponytail of the girl sitting in front of him. Then it flew up and over to the window, then back to the girl. Then, as it zipped upward with the strong lift of its wings, Oliver shot his hand out and snagged it in his fingers.

The familiar muffled buzz of the tiny fluttering thing banging around inside his closed fist made Oliver feel better.

Slowly, he slid his thumb to the side to look in at his latest victim. He was grinning at the thought of plucking off those tiny wings, when he realized he was being watched.

"What are you doing?" It was the kid next to him, whose name was Henry. He was a tallish boy with a faint hint of hair on his upper lip and a rash of red pimples on his chin. Henry had obviously begun his own nightmarish trip into adolescence with mixed results.

"Nothin'," mumbled Oliver, immediately putting his closed hand down on the desk. He'd already been labeled "new kid" and didn't need "fly boy" added to his name-calling list.

Oliver waited until Henry shrugged and went back to his math book. Safe at last, Oliver was just about to let the fly go, when he remembered Mooch. He'd forgotten to feed him, and this fly surely would be a yummy snack. Oliver slid his cupped hand back into his pocket—hiding the fly carefully inside.

"Five minutes to go." Oliver was back to watching the ticking clock. He couldn't wait to get home, and even though he had to paint the crummy kitchen all afternoon, it would be a welcome relief from the day he'd just had.

Oliver started preparing for his exodus and cleared his desk, first putting the gemstone back inside his pocket, then dropping his math book into his knapsack. He was just reaching for his pencil when a slow warmth began to spread through his leg.

For a split second, he flashed back to an embarrassing incident in kindergarten when he'd peed in his pants, and instinctively he looked down at his leg to check what was causing this feeling.

He was relieved to see he had full control of his bladder. But when he looked back up—things were far from okay. It was as if he were seeing everything in front of him through a prism—a multiviewed sight. Instead of one classroom clock on the wall, there were suddenly one hundred.

His stomach turned next, a nauseous feeling that shot straight through him. He stood up, interrupting the teacher in midsentence, and ran out of the room without explanation.

Racing down the empty hallway, he was still seeing a zillion images of everything, and he was getting pretty freaked out. The boys' room sign hovered in multiples in front of him, and he pushed the door open, hoping he'd make it to the toilet in time.

But the nausea disappeared as soon as he caught a glimpse of himself in the bathroom mirror. He stopped and stared into the glass at a hundred identical images that terrified and excited him at the same time.

Oliver was turning into a fly.

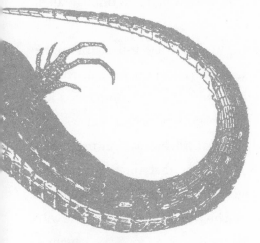

CHAPTER ELEVEN

"**D**ON'T YOU SEE? First the salamander child and now my nephew. It's just a matter of time before all of our species are captured, tortured, and who knows what else!"

The General's impassioned speech was slowly stirring the Pond Elders to action, and only he knew he was purposely fanning the fire of their greatest fear: another human had arrived to destroy the Pond.

"I don't need to tell you what happened last time," he continued, standing atop a pyramid of rock. "Humans want only one thing—to wipe us out!"

The General spread his wings wide and pointed toward the water. "It took us years to clean what took them months to ruin. I'm not sure we want to go through all of that again."

And then, knowing he had their full attention, he retold the story of what happened when the Alliance was first formed and the threat from Byron Trumble was real and deadly.

At first the newly formed Alliance was just an agreement between the Six Families that they would band together to survive. The food chain stayed in place; frogs slurped bugs, foxes feasted on fish—it was all just done with a bit more respect.

They were all on equal footing (and fin), so information was no longer hoarded like acorns for the long winter. What one Family knew was quickly shared with the other five. Skills were assessed and responsibilities assigned. For this reason it became the crows' task to fly surveillance missions over the paper mill and report back to the Alliance with whatever they saw. It was dangerous work. If the thick plumes of poisonous orange-green smoke coming from the factory didn't kill them, a blast from Byron Trumble's gun could.

Month after month the reports were consistent. The factory continued spewing filth that flowed into the river, over the waterfall and downstream into their Pond. Years went by and the harmful effects continued to spread. But one late spring day the crows returned with the news that the colored mess had stopped—the factory had been shut down. Simultaneously, Byron Trumble's appearance began to grow more haggard, as the man wandered outside dressed only in pajamas and his horrid white shoes, the deadly shotgun still by his side.

The Alliance learned that the factory had been forced to close (even crooked politicians can't protect you when you scam all your investors). The small house became Byron Trumble's only possession. Crazed and drunk most of the time, his aim became more erratic but no less lethal. The Alliance knew they had to do something, which is when they voted to drive the man off the property—or die trying.

The General knew the story well. They all did, which helped him use it to scare them all again. Yes, the Alliance had been successful all those years ago. They'd worked together and bombarded the man with a well-planned assault of stinging, biting, pooping, and clawing, which ensured that Byron Trumble would never return. And yes, they'd carried on the Alliance's mandate to ruin the house and chase off anyone who might attempt to occupy it.

But somehow things had gone horribly wrong. Another human family had been allowed to move in and The General, reminding them all of their history, was using it to further his own secret plan—to destroy the Alliance.

Mooch and Antoine's fate now lay in the hands of the

nervous Alliance members. The General smirked at how easy it all was.

The vote to leave Antoine to fend for himself was a no-brainer. He'd had military training. But despite the impassioned pleas and numerous arguments in favor of freeing Mooch, the group decision was to leave him in the house. His mother fainted. Several newts shouted their disapproval. And hidden behind a patch of ragweed, Willy scowled, already knowing that the Elders would never do anything to help get his best friend back.

"He may be just a child, but he may prove useful!" shouted Big Mama. "It is in our best interest to leave him with the humans and let him observe whatever it is they are up to."

"Great. Use him or lose him," thought Willy sourly. He was disgusted. Casting a final glance to the Elders, he turned his back on the gathering and flew off to do what he knew was right.

Puberty affects kids in different ways. Emotions go wild, hormones cause bodily changes—but the sudden appearance of wings and a thorax? That's not taught in health class.

Alone in the school bathroom, Oliver was getting used to seeing through the multilenses of his compound eyes. He watched as paper-thin, transparent wings sprouted from his shoulder blades. A throbbing headache accompanied the thick, feeler-like hairs that were beginning to rise out of his head, which had begun to reshape itself into the unmistakable form of a fly's. It was total sci-fi morph stuff, and it was actually happening to *him*; it was his own personal horror movie. He couldn't take his eyes away. He watched as his mouth formed into a fly's elongated proboscis and his arms shriveled into one of three pairs of appendages.

How can this be happening? he thought, petrified and thrilled and curious all at the same time. His insides vibrated with molecular change. Cells were dividing into new road maps of DNA that were changing a boy into a bug.

"Shut up and get in there!" Oliver heard the bathroom door opening, and he freaked out. Maybe he was having a strange feverish reaction to the school lunch, or maybe this really was somehow happening, but either way, he knew he didn't want anyone to see him like this.

The sudden adrenaline rush caused his heart to beat so fast that his whole head echoed with the thud-thudding sound of his frantic pulse. Sweat poured from his bug/boy body, and a split second later the room spun into a dizzying blur.

The next thing he knew, Oliver was a fraction of his regular size, high above the bathroom, staring down at the same two bullies who had tried to extort money from him just hours earlier.

He felt the rapid humming vibration of wings where

his shoulders used to be and the exhilaration of being suspended in midair.

"I'm flying!" he shouted, now dipping and diving and buzzing in semicircles.

"Ow! Cut it out!"

Looking down, Oliver saw that the bullies were hitting on another easy target, a mousy orange-haired boy they'd cornered against the sinks.

"Come on, Chester, cough it up." It was the larger kid doing the talking, while his wiry accomplice snickered with asthmatic glee, keeping watch by the heavy door.

"Listen, Larry. I am fully prepared to make restitution," the kid whimpered. "But it's the first day. I wasn't anticipating being held accountable yet."

In response, Larry grabbed the kid by his striped sweater-vest and slapped him in the face with his meaty hand.

"That's for using words I don't understand," said the thug with a thin smile. "And *this* is for not paying up." Larry kneed Chester in his groin, causing the boy to drop to the ground in pain.

Oliver felt sympathy for the kid sprawled out on the bathroom floor. The same fate might soon enough be his.

The bell rang—the day was over. Finally. On their way out, Larry and his sidekick laughed as they threw a couple of wads of wet paper towel at Chester.

"You owe us. Tomorrow. Double or trouble," snarled

Larry. *Thwack.* A wet clump caught Chester in the forehead, making him look even more pathetic.

Oliver thought of trying to make the kid feel better or rushing off to tell someone what had just happened, but then he remembered he was no longer a member of the human race. Like it or not, he was a fly. A tiny, powerless fly.

Oliver landed on the bathroom stall door, amazed at how his sticky padded feet clung effortlessly to the vertical surface. He watched Chester get up and wash his face with cold water and calmly comb his hair back with his fingers.

"It's gonna be a long year," the boy mumbled to his reflection before limping out of the bathroom.

Finally alone, Oliver swooped over to the mirrors and got a good look at himself. It took him a moment to focus, but there he was—a puny, ugly, kind of frightening fly. Gone was his slightly lazy left eye, the overbite, the tiny scar on his cheek from when Rachel threw a Chatty Chyna doll at him when she was seven. In fact, all the physical things that made Oliver who he was were erased and replaced by something he had no idea how to explain. And if he couldn't explain *how* it had happened, he had no idea how to reverse it!

He paced nervously, trying to come up with a plan to get back to his normal self. Maybe it had something to do with the gem—but he didn't have the gem because he didn't have pants, or pockets or . . . Oh, man! I am way sunk, he thought. What if this was it and he had to stay a fly forever . . . or until some rolled-up newspaper swatted him into mush, or some kid like him grabbed him and tried snapping off his wings! He suddenly felt sick. Sicker than he'd ever felt in his whole life. He wanted to cry but wasn't even sure if flies had tear ducts.

After what felt like forever, he finally landed on the ledge of the sink and took a deep breath. Instinctively he started to eat a boulder-sized cookie crumb, which would've tasted great if the sight of his fly proboscis making a paste out of the snack hadn't totally grossed him out. And that's when the simplest idea popped into his mind. He closed his bulging eyes tight and wished he could be himself again.

His head filled with noise. The room spun. His thoughts became blurs of memory and colorful light.

A heartbeat later—there he was. Fully clothed. No wings. No body hair. Just one hundred percent lazy-eyed, under-biting, cheek-scarred Oliver. He rummaged inside his pants pockets and removed the bright golden gem. Was this the cause? He had no idea, and no time to think about that now. His watch was beeping—reminding him that school was out and he had to catch a ride home.

Mooch was napping. His dreams were colorless and filled with distant memories of hanging out beneath a tree, where he used to dig up beetles and ladybugs and swallow them whole, listening as they cried out to be spared so appetizing a death.

Antoine's wing still hurt, but each day he tried to move it just a little more past the point of pain. He knew from his boot camp training that he needed to exercise the appendage before it mended in a crooked useless flap of feathers. It was the first time anything from his squadron lessons had proven even remotely useful.

Willy hovered outside the bedroom window, looking for a way to get in. If the Alliance wouldn't help save Mooch, then he would, somehow. The only problem was, Indoors was foreign territory to him, and a world without trees and shrubs made him nervous.

"Well, who have we here?" said Antoine as he watched Willy ease his long dragonfly body through a rip in the window screen.

"Tell ya what. You're either breakfast, lunch, or dinner. I'll let *you* pick." Antoine laughed as he stalked Willy with his watchful dark eyes.

Willy ignored the crow. He was too busy trying to get Mooch's attention. He clicked his long legs on the aquarium glass, but Mooch was lost to his dreams.

"You ain't gonna rouse him that way," continued Antoine, glad to have someone to talk to. "I should know. We're practically like brothers—identical twins. Except he can't fly. Well, actually, neither can I. Hey, lemme tell you 'bout my wing. . . ."

It had taken Antoine approximately twenty-two seconds to drive Willy completely crazy. The dragonfly flew over to Antoine's rusty cage, being careful not to get too close. This nutty bird might actually eat him.

"Listen, whoever you are. I think I know Mooch a little better than you. That salamander and I go way back and . . ."

Antoine's eyes lit up. "Oh. You must be that Willy guy. Yeah, Mooch talks about you all the time."

Willy smiled and felt a warm glow of friendship. But Antoine continued.

"Sure. You're the dude who got him into this crazy mess. Yup. I've heard all about you."

It was true that Antoine knew about Willy. Mooch didn't talk much, but when he did, it was with a mixture of excitement and sadness about the friend who'd dumped him, taken him back, and then hurt him all over again.

Willy didn't know what to say. His feelings were wounded by a stranger with a big mouth, and big mouths often speak the truth. He felt uncomfortable and wanted to leave as fast as he could.

"*Snrtzzzzgrrr.*"

The wet snorting noise Mooch made in his sleep brought Willy back to his mission, and he whizzed away from Antoine and over to the glass aquarium. This time he noticed that the lid on top was askew, so he flew inside and landed on the foul-smelling gravel next to sleepy Mooch.

"Mooch . . . buddy . . . it's me. Willy."

The whispers did nothing. Mooch was a heavy sleeper.

Willy tried again, a little louder. "Come on, pal. Time to get off your butt and get out of here."

Antoine rolled his eyes. This guy was way too nice. "Yo, Plumpso!" the crow shrieked as loud as he could. "Get your chubby self up! *Cawwwwwww!*"

Mooch shot awake. Willy hoped his ears would stop ringing someday.

Antoine just smiled. "Works every time."

The fog lifted from Mooch's dream state, and the salamander's eyes focused on the dragonfly.

"Willy? What are you . . . Wait, I'm dreaming, right?"

"Nope. You're awake. I'm here to take you home." Willy felt like a hero.

There was only one problem: Mooch didn't want to be rescued.

"Home? No thanks." Mooch turned away, looking for something to eat.

"Gimme a break, Mooch," Willy said as he flew around the perimeter of the cage. "You can't live like this."

But Mooch liked his new pad. And he still hadn't totally forgiven Willy. He wasn't ready to give him the satisfaction of a renewed friendship.

"No thanks," Mooch said coldly. "I'm perfectly happy here."

"Man, you are the most stubborn dude I know," huffed Willy. "Don't you get it? This isn't natural!"

"Maybe not for you, Willy, *Mr. Bug-boss.*" Mooch knew that the sarcasm stung Willy, but he needed to say it. "I like it here. It's . . . nice."

"Nice?" Willy looked around Mooch's cage. "You can't breathe in here. There's no food. And drinks . . . ?" He sipped the water in Mooch's dish, which hadn't been changed in a week.

"Acccckkk!" Willy choked, spewing the disgusting water all over the gravel. "You can't live like this. I'm busting you out."

"You and what army?" asked Antoine, perched by the bars of his cage.

Both Mooch and Willy knew exactly which army he'd use. Before Mooch could stop him, Willy had flown out of the aquarium, through the window, and had disappeared back into the fresh air.

The car ride home was filled with the typical "how was school" questions and the equally typical sullen, monosyllabic answers. Rachel had hated her day—no surprise. And Oliver, so wrapped up in what he'd just experienced, stared silently out the window, trying to piece together how and why he'd just become an insect.

Later that afternoon, Oliver began painting the kitchen. But he could not stop thinking about what had happened to him, and he was completely distracted. Needless to say, he made a total mess of the job.

Finally, after the brushes were cleaned and the spilled paint was wiped up, and after he'd promised to redo it all on Saturday, Oliver ran up the stairs to the quiet of his room.

Mooch was thrilled. Finally. He'd be fed.

"You ready to stop complaining, fat boy?" shouted Antoine from his cage. "Here comes the grub!"

But Oliver had no mind for feeding either of his pets. He was transfixed by the gem in his hand—by its amber glow and the strange possibilities it possessed. The power it held was far more compelling than any food—with the exception of the handful of candy fireballs he'd loaded up on to get him through what he figured would be a long night ahead.

CHAPTER TWELVE

JUST TWO WEEKS had gone by since school had started; two weeks since Oliver had suddenly and quite by accident turned into a fly. He still had no idea exactly what the gem was—but by now he sure knew what it could do. And how to use it!

Keeping such a marvelous secret made him feel like he would burst. But who would believe him anyway? He kept his mouth shut and knew he had to be careful not to behave too out of the ordinary or he would somehow blow it all. That's why he'd been doing his homework—but not all of it; keeping his room clean—just sort of; and staying out of his sister's way—totally!

Two weeks ago Oliver had closed his bedroom door, and everything he knew about the world had changed. . . .

Figuring out how the magic worked had taken that whole first night. Mooch had long given up on the prospect of being fed and was snoring softly and hungrily, curled against the corner of the glass. But Antoine was fascinated. His attention was glued to Oliver and his weird shiny jewel.

There's something strange about that thing, the crow thought.

He fought off his need for sleep by banging his head against the side of the cage whenever he felt his eyes start to droop. It hurt a lot, but it kept him alert and awake, and only slightly dizzy.

For Oliver, it was the adrenaline-fueled excitement that kept him awake. He rolled the gem in his palm, feeling each edge, memorizing the shape. He examined it with a magnifying glass, looking deeply into the strange imperfections in hopes of finding a clue. He even spent an hour on the Internet trying to discover what kind of crystal it might be. He determined that he had found some sort of beryl crystal; at least that's what it most resembled. But that was just a "fact," and didn't help at all in discovering the secret of what the thing *really* was.

As the hours slipped past midnight, his mind flooded with wild ideas and fantasies of how he could use the magic to do incredible things. For a kid who'd played it safe all his life, he was suddenly ready to jump headfirst into something totally unknown, which filled him with an excitement he'd never felt.

But there was another feeling lurking in his gut: fear. What if he *did* figure out the secret, but he got trapped in a one-way trip with no way to return?

"That'd be just my luck," Oliver said, lying on his bed staring up at the ceiling. "Spending the rest of my life as a dung beetle."

For that reason he decided that, before going any further, he'd leave a trail of breadcrumbs behind so someone could follow, or at least know what had happened to him.

With the crow watching, he ripped a sheet of yellow lined paper out of his school notebook and, uncapping his favorite felt-tipped pen, he began:

To Whom It May Concern:
If you are reading this, I am probably not a kid anymore and am in deep trouble. I know it sounds crazy, but most likely I am some sort of bug or animal right now. Whatever you do, don't squish ants or flush any spiders down the toilet. I guess I could also be a chair, so please don't sit on any furniture that looks like me. I don't know how it

happened—but I am sorry if I left my room a mess (Mom) or still owe you five bucks (Rachel). This is all because of a yellow crystal-thing I found when I broke the roof. Guess I screwed up again.

Love, Oliver

He knew the note would probably never be needed, and that it sounded absolutely nuts, but what the heck—better safe than sorry. Oliver folded the letter in half, slid it inside his desk drawer, and turned his attention back to trying to learn the secret of the magic.

For two full hours that night Oliver used the gem as a wishing stone. He held it in a clenched fist, eyes shut tightly, his inner voice chanting, I *wish I was a fly. I wish I was a dog. I wish I had a Big Mac with large fries and a Coke.* Nothing.

He then tried rubbing the gem over and over, hoping that a genie-like magic might happen. All he got from that was a nasty blister on his finger.

Trying to re-create his transformation in school, he even placed the gem in his pocket and held a freshly nabbed fly in his hand. But he didn't get even the slightest hint of anything strange happening, and he decided to take a break.

Antoine was exhausted and had quite a headache from repeatedly hitting his head on the cage. Daybreak wasn't far off; he'd force himself to make it that long. The crow yawned, watching as Oliver picked up Mooch and carried the still-sleeping salamander over to the window, where the first rays of sun were just beginning to streak brightly on the glass. Outside, the pond was smooth as a mirror, reflecting the amber-gray sky, and a thin mist hovered above the surface.

"Must be kinda nice to live out there," said Oliver softly, admiring how pretty the pond was at this time of day. And for the first time, he actually felt guilty for plucking the salamander from his natural surroundings.

Mooch squinted as a narrow shaft of sun forced him awake. Slowly the Pond came into view, and as he focused his sleepy eyes on his former home, a lump rose in his throat. Everything he'd told Willy—about being happy living inside his man-made cage—suddenly felt like a lie. He missed the Pond and the woods and the smell of pine needles. He longed to feel the fresh air on his slippery skin again, a realization that took him quite by surprise.

"Hey li'l guy, I got a snack for you," Oliver said, remembering the fly he'd just caught. And like a hook, the word "snack" instantly caught and yanked Mooch away from his homesickness.

Oliver fed the starving salamander and then rubbed his soft belly, and together they watched the golden sunrise spread, as if from an artist's brush, across the

Pond and woods beyond. A single Canada goose, already sensing the preview of winter's chill, glided with a wing-flapping splash onto the water, one of his last stops of the season.

Oliver decided to take the gem from his pocket and see what the light would look like fractured through the golden stone. Mooch was still staring longingly at the Pond, watching a wake-up ritual he knew so well. Pickerel and trout were just beginning to break the calm surface in search for bug breakfasts. Robins and wrens were trading insults—masked as trilling songs. Frogs punctuated the music with deep-bellied belches. Mooch watched it all fondly.

But Antoine had seen enough. His eyelids fluttered. He needed sleep and had just decided to call it quits, when Oliver held the gemstone to the window. A diffracted ray of yellow light shone through the stone and lit the opposite wall in a speckled pattern that shot up to the ceiling and then cascaded down along the floor.

"Wow," sighed the crow.

Oliver gripped the stone in his right hand while Mooch sat comfortably in his left. "Look, lizard, look at the light." He put the stone right up to Mooch's face so that he too could see the world golden and warm.

The instant the gem touched the salamander, it happened: the room spun and Oliver had just enough time to register surprise before both he and Mooch were on the floor staring eye to eye. Salamander to salamander.

Antoine couldn't believe what he'd just seen. He had to bang his head three times against the cage to make sure he was really still awake.

"I get it! I get it!" Oliver shouted as a salamander now lying on the floor next to Mooch. "It wasn't enough for me to touch the gem. *You* needed to touch it too!"

The key to the magic was found. It was like a triangle, a complete electrical circuit—three things that all needed to be connected together. Back at school it had worked when the gem was touching both him *and* the fly in his pocket.

"I'm a lizard!" Oliver shouted as he ran in a circle, trying to turn his head enough to get a good look at his new body. He rolled onto his back and wiggled his webbed toes.

Oliver suddenly stopped celebrating. Something bothered him. Why had the change happened so quickly this time? With the fly at school, it had happened gradually, not all at once. And then Oliver remembered that earlier, the fly was hurt and barely still alive in his hand. Maybe that affected the speed of the transformation.

Mooch was so shocked, he felt like he hadn't blinked in minutes. Finally he spoke. "What is going on here? Who are you?"

Oliver couldn't believe it. Did he just understand

animal-talk? He gazed with awe at Mooch. "Lizard, you talk? You. *Talk!*"

"Duh. I can also count to ten by twos," Mooch snapped back. "Talking is easy. What just happened here—now *that* seems like the tough one."

Oliver tried explaining what he knew to Mooch. In turn, Mooch told Oliver that he wasn't a lizard but a salamander. That his name was Mooch. And that he was still very, very hungry.

"*Hungry?* Oh, man! I haven't fed you for hours!" said Oliver apologetically.

"Hours? With the exception of that measly fly, try all yesterday," replied Mooch. "And all last night!"

Oliver nodded his small head. "No problem, Mooch. I'll just go to my desk and grab you some . . ."

Oliver stopped in midsentence. He couldn't just grab some food for the hungry salamander. His desk was a massive mountain that loomed high above him.

Remembering what he did back in the bathroom at school, he shut his salamander eyes tight and wished to be himself again. Instantly came the swirling sound like a tornado's twisting wind, and again—as suddenly as he'd slid into the amphibian's body—he was himself, sitting cross-legged next to Mooch.

Once again he was holding the remarkable crystal, and he looked at it with even more appreciation than ever.

Though Oliver was now completely satisfied that he

knew how to travel in both directions, this last change was too much for the bewildered Antoine. The crow blinked his eyes repeatedly and then dunked his whole head into the water dish.

Over the next week Oliver tested the gem's power. He now wore the crystal on a piece of leather around his neck so it would always be close to him. For safety, he also decided to use only Mooch for his magical experiments. Later he could try transforming into other animals, but for now he wanted to stick with what he knew worked.

It was a learning process for both of them. Mooch had always been curious about humans, and Oliver wanted to know everything he could about salamanders.

"You're born in the water? No way!"

"Yup," Mooch answered. "But explain this one: boys really go the bathroom standing up? That's freaky."

"Trust me. After a supersized soda you'd be happy it's so easy." Oliver smiled, and then remembered something he'd read in the school library. "What's the deal with your body making mucus to keep your skin moist? That sounds totally disgusting."

Mooch grinned. "Not as disgusting as you making mucus just to spit onto the sidewalk!"

"Point taken," Oliver laughed, then gave Mooch a damp, web-toed high five.

* * *

The big day had finally arrived. After five cautious experiments—the longest Oliver stayed a salamander was fifteen minutes, and the farthest the two ventured from the bedroom was the kitchen (to wolf down the leftover meat loaf that Oliver, as a boy, had hidden behind the door)—they took the big trip. The trip outside.

Oliver was nervous about leaving the house. But Mooch was excited and anxious to be in the fresh air again. He wasn't planning to return to the house. He had said a silent adios to the annoying crow, because he'd planned to escape—after he showed Oliver around the Pond, of course. He owed the kid that much.

The two salamanders stood on the wooden landing of the creaky porch, each observing the night. It was mid-September and the air already had a fresh, cool snap to it—a reminder of the fall that would soon descend on the Pond. The new moon was a few days off and a silver hook hung low and bright in the clear sky.

"Mmm, it is so wonderful!" Mooch said, taking a nice long sip of the air. He couldn't believe he was free, and he had to restrain himself from bolting off into the woods and away from the human, or salamander, or . . . whatever Oliver was.

Oliver, on the other hand, was overwhelmed. It was one thing to be a small creature inside a house, but stepping outside and looking up at the bigness of the world took his breath away.

"It's all so . . . *huge!*" he said, staring out at the never-ending night.

And as he took his first tentative steps into the wet grass, he knew there was no turning back—his real adventures were about to begin.

CHAPTER THIRTEEN

WILLY WAS FURIOUS. Roxanne had just accused him of being jealous of Mooch's friendship with the new salamander at the Pond.

"Jealous? *Of that four-legged runt?* Get over yourself." He snorted as the two flew a crazy flight pattern among the remaining leaves that still clung to the trees. She wasn't going to ruin the first fun he'd had in weeks, he thought as he whipped through milkweed stalks, exploding their white furry sacks into tiny floating parachutes.

"Well," the fly said with a sneer, dodging a pinecone

that hung just below the branch of a fragrant evergreen. "I guess I'm way off base. You must be this bent outta shape just because you're about to smack into a . . ."

"Ooof!"

Too late. Willy was so busy denying his hurt feelings that he flew directly into a pinecone.

Embarrassed and a little wobbly, Willy insisted he'd meant to do that. Roxanne couldn't help but laugh.

The truth was, however, that Willy *was* mad and hurt and confused. At first, seeing Mooch free of the house and that awful cage made him feel great. Finally, Mooch was coming to his senses. But even from a distance Willy saw that Mooch had a new friend, another *salamander*, which shocked Willy because he knew that Mooch had never wanted to hang out with other salamanders. Or more to the point, they'd never wanted to hang with *him*.

After a few days of watching from afar, Willy finally flew down to Mooch, resolved to try and patch things up with his old friend.

"Dude!" he called out with a huge smile.

But Mooch's own grin dropped as soon as he saw Willy. He and his new "buddy" were in the middle of a rousing game of shadow tag and apparently didn't want to be interrupted. That, or Mooch was still really angered by what Willy had done to get him captured.

Willy picked up on the vibe instantly. And that other salamander, man, what was his problem? Staring at Willy like he'd never seen a dragonfly before. Jeesh, what a weirdo. And then Mooch, just like that, said they were late for "something," clearly blowing Willy off like they'd never been best friends.

So sure, maybe Willy was jealous. But he'd never admit that. Not to a fly, and certainly not to Mooch. But deep down he knew the truth: that the only way to get his old friend back would be by force.

"Listen up! Our mission will begin at sundown," Willy commanded a smallish group of Japanese beetles standing in the shade of a sunflower. "We invade the house and go straight for the salamander upstairs. Got it?"

"Give it a rest, Willy." That reaction came from a meal-worm, who, like the other kids, had only attended the impromptu meeting because Willy had promised snacks.

"Where's the food, man?" shouted the others. "Who cares about a stupid mission?"

"Yeah, your Alliance thing was so last month."

"Lo-ser!"

Willy's grip on the insect kids was gone. They'd had enough of his secret plans and bullheaded orders, and as soon as Willy admitted that he hadn't brought anything to eat, they'd had enough of him too.

"You do good work, Françoise," The General said, poking at three dead trout whose once-colorful scales were already losing their shine.

Françoise was a small, red fox who spoke with a distinctive French accent even though she'd been born and raised in the nearby woods. She answered proudly, "Yes, zis is what I do, *mon cher*. Look closely. Zere are no marks of my claws. No evidence at all zat zey were caught and killed by *moi*."

"Yes," The General hissed happily. "Not killed at all. Just dead. Mysteriously, unmistakably dead."

The satisfied General looked from the fish to the fox. "Just don't get too used to the thrill, Françoise." He leaned closer, his breath rank and sour. "It'll get inside you until your entire life becomes consumed by death."

The General smiled as he narrowed his gaze, and the fox was almost certain she saw his dark eyes glow bloodred before he kicked the lifeless fish into the Pond's shallow pool.

A moment later he was gone, flapping his massive wings. The fox sighed in relief that she was rid of The General's uncomfortable presence. But a heartbeat later The General swooped back down, narrowly missing her ear tips with his hot whispering beak.

"And Françoise, breathe one word of this to *anyone* and you'll truly be swimming with the fishes. The dead ones."

And then he was gone. This time for good.

"Um. The Boston Tea Party?"

Oliver was grasping at straws. He not only hadn't

heard the question but wasn't even positive which of his five classes he was in. Taking a chance, he'd pulled a history answer out of thin air. But he could've said anything and had a better shot at being right.

The familiar laughter of the class made Oliver sink deeper into his chair.

Mrs. Wippet pushed her glasses back onto her long hook of a nose. "A joke? Is this that?" She spoke in clipped, backward-sounding sentences. Now he realized that this wasn't his history class, but English.

"Stand. Listen to what is said." She was now hovering over him, and in her huge, bright green dress she resembled a giant balloon, the kind that floated in Thanksgiving parades. Oliver prayed she would just pop, or better still, blow away.

Instead, he rose to his feet as the giggles and whispers continued around him.

"Paying attention. We do. Clear? Obtuse? Which?"

"Clear," he said, staring straight at her eyes, which were magnified by her thick glasses. If she had ever blinked she must have done it at home or in the safety of the teachers' lounge, because he swore he'd never seen her do it in class.

"Where your mind is, I do not know." Mrs. Wippet turned on her heels and waddled back to her desktop fortress as Oliver sank into the safety of his hard chair.

She faced the class and redirected the question to everyone. "Rhyming couplets? Who can recite?"

School was never a favorite on Oliver's top-ten places to spend time. Still, between the upheaval of the move and the distraction of his magic gem, this school year was off to a particularly rocky start.

He'd already had one parent-principal conference, two detentions, and eight shakedowns for money by Larry and his nasal sidekick, whose nickname he'd learned was "Snot." What Oliver didn't have—in school, anyway—was a friend. A kid who got his jokes or waved hello in the hall.

Oliver had been lonely his whole life. His experience had taught him that real kids could never compete with the intimate companions on his television. The characters that appeared in colored pixels on his twenty-one-inch screen never disappointed him. Or called him names. Or arranged playdates with him and never showed up.

When he was six, he had his first and only best friend, a real buddy named Marco Jasper. They'd met on the first day of kindergarten, both showing up wearing the same Poké-mon T-shirt. Their bond was made among paste and colored paper and nap times on blankets by the fish tank. For Oliver (and his grateful mother) it was the best time of his life.

Unfortunately, it had only lasted one year—until a job transfer sent Marco's family far away. Oliver was devastated but soon slipped into the comfortable habit of being alone. Holed up by himself, watching TV, he could hang tight to the idea that everything was just fine. Keeping to himself had become something he started to actually enjoy.

Until now. School may have been lonely, but life at home was getting better every day.

"Careful, these rocks are slippery when the moss gets wet."

Mooch was demonstrating his Pond knowledge by showing Oliver some of his favorite places to play and nap. He had given up on the idea of running away from Oliver. He was having way too much fun.

The two salamanders were perched on top of the highest rock that bordered the muddy shallows of the Pond. In the summer, when the heat baked this pocket of water all afternoon, the mud was warm and soothingly smooth to lay on. But in the fall, the mud was cool and silken, and the water was just chilly enough to snap you to attention.

"Now, here's the fun part. . . ." Mooch took one step on the mossy rock, and—*ziiip*—he was sliding down its steep side all the way to the water, where he landed with a loud, wet *slap*.

"Fancy dive, huh?" he yelled as soon as his head broke the surface.

"More like a belly flop," called Oliver, laughing as he tested the top of the rock with his own foot before slipping on the moss and sliding headfirst into the Pond.

Splash!

The surprise of being underwater frightened Oliver at first, but his elongated amphibian body reacted differently from his upright human one. His tail acted like a rudder and his webbed toes were like flippers that propelled him in whatever direction he chose to go.

"Hey! You're getting the hang of the extra appendage thing. Way to go, Ollie." Mooch said as soon as Oliver's head popped above the water.

"What do you expect? I'm a fast learner," Oliver replied. Strangely, he was more comfortable in this slithery skin than in his own human one.

Mooch grinned, then squirted Oliver with a big mouthful of pond water. "You mean . . . I'm a great teacher!"

Mooch had always thought of himself as a follower, a hanger-on, the one who needed to be told stuff like which droppings belonged to which animals and which tracks meant trouble. But with Oliver by his side, he was the designated know-it-all, and he was surprising himself with all that he actually knew.

Mooch was happy with his new friend. It was a different friendship than the one he used to have with bold, outspoken Willy. He and Oliver were the same, in quiet temperament and in slimy skin. Of course, if he had stopped for a second to think, he'd have realized how temporary this situation really was. Oliver had used some sort of magic to become a salamander, and he could very well use the same magic to become a hungry owl, or menacing bear, or any species higher up the food chain. And not only would that destroy the friendship, it would most likely make a meal out of Mooch.

But none of that bothered Mooch today. He and Oliver were out in the cool bright sun, playing in the Pond and breathing air that didn't reek of gravel and stale leftover food.

Mooch liked the deal he had with Oliver: he'd live in the boy's room if Oliver promised to play outside every day. These were easy promises for each to make, because they both needed a friend more than anything else.

CHAPTER FOURTEEN

"**W**AKEY-WAKEY!"

"No," the two voices replied groggily.

"Come on, sun's up. Sky's blue. Let's go, go, go!" The crow rattled the bars with his beak and paced his cage for the hundredth time since dawn.

"Hey, who died and made you a rooster?" Mooch yawned from under the rock in his cage. "Shut yer yappin' trap already!"

Antoine acted hurt, though in reality this drama was played out daily, with some minor changes to the script at every performance.

"Hey, I'm a product of my environment," he answered. "In the military we were up with the sun every morning."

The crow saluted, using his "hurt" wing, then quickly switched to the other one, just in case Oliver's mother walked in.

Fearful of being set free, Antoine had been doing his best to hide the fact that his wing was totally healed. It had felt fine for about two weeks, but whenever Carol came in to inspect his medical progress, he limped. He drooped. He fainted onto the newspaper-lined floor, pretending a surge of pain had just made him black out. And each time, she just shook her head, wondering why a simple break was taking so long to mend.

Antoine knew he had a good thing going in the kid's room and was in no rush to run into his crazy uncle.

"You asked for it. I'm gonna sing!" This was the thing both Mooch and Oliver dreaded most. Not only did the crow sing like a *crow*—but his songs were ridiculous, atonal nonsense.

"Sky so blue, river of mud. Gimme, gimme pancake time. I have a hangnail." The song was mind-numbingly awful.

"An-toine, please?" Oliver groaned into the pillow, almost wishing he still couldn't understand the crow.

Since Oliver had first become a salamander and talked to Mooch, interactions like this were happening every day. He now understood all the creatures around him, even

when he was in his human form. And they could understand him. It was as if some switch in his brain had been
tripped and all the channels were open all the time—for
better and, especially now, for worse.

In the room next door, Rachel banged on the wall with
her fist, another part of the morning ritual that Oliver and
Mooch would have gladly done without.

"Shut that crow up!" she shrieked from the other side
of the ugly striped wallpaper. "You do it, or I will!"

Of course, in response, Rachel heard only: "*Cawwww
crrrr cawcawww awwww!*" But for Mooch and Oliver, the
crow's response was quite clear: "Lemme at her! I'll show
her a new way to pierce her ears!"

Oliver threw a dirty sock at the birdcage. Antoine
tripped over his own claws and fell into the water dish.

"Fine. I'll shut up," Antoine said as he shook his tail
feathers, spraying water around the room. "I just thought
you'd want to get an early start."

And then Oliver remembered. This wasn't Antoine's
typical, annoying wake-up call. It was Saturday, the day
Antoine was going to teach him how to fly!

Pudge felt like he was about to hurl. Nothing ruins a sushi
breakfast faster than the sight of bloated, decomposed fish.
It was one thing to stalk a slippery-finned trout and kill it
with a quick jab of your own sharp claws, but seeing the
rotted, stinky carcass of another trout, well that was

enough to turn even the most voracious carnivore into a vegetarian.

The raccoon held his stomach and ran off to inform the Alliance. It was happening again. The Pond was becoming polluted.

Lester Biggs had a headache the size of a redwood. He'd been banging out the news all morning, and even though he was finally done, his insides still reverberated like a Chinese gong.

"I'm getting too old for this," the woodpecker lamented as he dipped his whole head into the cool water of the brook. For the millionth time, Lester wished he were any other bird, animal, or inanimate object that didn't have the ridiculous job of knocking his beak against the hard wood of a tree.

But it was his job, and fortunately for everyone, he did it well. An emergency session of the Alliance was planned for later that afternoon, and the entire Pond was abuzz.

Everyone was curious. Everyone, that is, except the young crow perched on a second-story windowsill of the house, who seemed too scared to even blink.

"I can't," said the crow, staring down at the ground. "It won't work."

Antoine flapped down from the nearby tree branch to the ledge of the window. "Great. So you'll pal around on your four little feet with chubby over there at the drop of a hat, but when it comes to a little high flying with the crow—it's 'no siree.' Well, don't that beat all."

It was true. Oliver had been talking about flying all week, but now he wanted to call the whole thing off. It wasn't that being a crow was any less interesting than being a salamander. In fact, the transformation into a crow had been smooth, and he felt instantly comfortable inside his feathered body, marveling at how his whole center of gravity was different from anything he'd felt as a person. His thin legs acted like pivots; the knee hinges worked backward! Walking felt a bit mechanical, as if he were some sort of windup toy.

Looking in the mirror, he had to smile at the sight of his new sleek shape, and as he held his wings open he felt like some sort of superhero. "The Amazing Crowman!" He liked that.

What he didn't like was the image of his black shiny body sprawled out on the ground below his window, broken and bent and most likely dead.

"It's like I told you before, just spread your wings open. The air will take over. You can't fail."

Antoine felt annoyed and realized how his teachers must've felt about his own timid approach to everything.

"Nope. Can't do it. Sorry, Antoine, but I'm gonna change back."

Antoine put a comforting wing around Oliver. "If that's what you need to do, then don't let me stop you."

Oliver smiled. "Thanks. Maybe another time."

"Sure, kid, we'll try again. Just one thing, though . . ."

"What?" Oliver turned to look at Antoine.

"Don't hate me for doing *this*." Antoine winced as he pushed Oliver off the windowsill.

Oliver fell fast. There was no time to be angry. His mind went blank as he watched the ground rush closer and closer. It was all happening quickly and yet in slow motion at the same time.

"Just open your wings!" Antoine called out. Oliver felt his wings lift from his body just as he'd done in countless flying dreams. His wingspan caught the rushing air and he swooped upward, aiming at the sky.

"I'm flying!" he shouted as Antoine joined him in flight. "You nearly killed me, you crazy crow!"

The crow glided into a lazy loop and slapped Oliver on the back. "What can I tell ya? When the going gets tough—the tough get pushed."

The General was picking at his lunch. Or more accurately, he was chasing it into a corner—where he planned to pluck the mouse into his beak with one gulp. But first, he'd scare it half to death. What fun!

"I do so love playing with my food," he said with delicious malice. The General pressed forward so that the quivering mouse was trapped against the stones of the cliff wall.

"*Cawwwwwwwwwwww!*" The sudden screech of

another crow startled The General. In that split second of lost concentration the mouse raced between his captor's legs and into the tangled brush of the woods.

The General burned with fury. What idiot had caused him to lose his lunch? He leaped into the air to give chase—and then it all made sense.

Flying in the near distance were two young crows. One had the unmistakable wing-flap of his ridiculous nephew. The General followed them discreetly, trying to see who the other awkward flyer was.

As he got closer, something inside him sensed trouble. What was it about that other crow that was so vaguely familiar? It made him feel unsettled and momentarily unsure of the plan that he'd been putting into motion for months. And that alone made him want to squish the punk.

The woodpecker's knocking message reminded The General that the Alliance meeting was about to start. This situation with the new crow would have to wait. He had more important business to attend to.

Oliver's fear of heights melted away with each flap of his wings. Antoine had been right. His instincts had taken over and now flying seemed natural and simple. After twenty minutes in the air, Oliver figured that flying was as easy as riding a bike—minus the being-on-solid-ground part.

Of course, as Antoine reminded him, there were certain things always to keep in mind: air currents, wing position, weather. But Oliver was too busy enjoying the view to pay close attention to his flight instructor's advice.

"The thing about a headwind," cautioned Antoine as they dove through some high maple branches, "it usually signals an upcoming shift in the weather. So when you feel that cold upper air sinking and warm moist air rising—watch out. It's thunderstorm time!"

But Oliver heard only the wind rushing in his ears. The sounds of the sky became as exciting as the feeling in his heart—the feeling of absolute freedom. To thwart gravity and experience the thrill of sailing through the invisible sky made him feel absolutely weightless. Gliding on a current of air with wings extended was better than any amusement park ride he'd ever been on. No roller coaster in the world would ever compete with the sudden drop that occurred when he tugged his wings close to his body, a straight sharp dive that he could pull out of by opening his wings and lifting his head back to the sky.

They soared around the perimeter of the Pond, circled over his tiny house below, and raced a falling leaf as it blew off a branch into the stiff afternoon breeze.

"So what do you think now, kiddo?" shouted Antoine as he glided side by side with Oliver. "Walking is so overrated, ain't it?"

Oliver smiled back. "I may never want to be a person

again. This is the best day of my life!"

"Make sure you tell that to salamander-boy. I like rubbing it in. Hey, you hungry?"

"Starved!"

"Great," said Antoine, grinning. "I know just the place to tantalize the taste buds. Follow me."

Antoine arced left, circling slowly away from the Pond. Oliver followed, showing off with a quick spiraling loop and nearly knocking into two blue jays, who were not at all impressed.

"I told you—swerve up!" screamed Max, the male jay.

"You said down. I heard down, so I went down!" Doris, as usual was right, or at least insisted she was, which only fueled their argument. "Next time, Max, we ask for directions!"

Oliver flew close behind Antoine, using the wake of his friend's body to glide effortlessly. Perhaps he was following too close, as a sudden foul odor filled Oliver's nose. He gagged.

"Phew! Next time give a warning before you cut one, huh, Antoine?"

"Hey, when I let one go, you'll know it." The crow laughed.

Oliver flew next to his friend, but still couldn't shake the awful, ripe smell. "Well, if it wasn't you, what is that horrible stink?"

Antoine grinned. "That, my friend . . . is lunch!" He

nodded toward the Little Falls garbage dump.

"Hope you're hungry," Antoine said as he began his descent. "They've got the best trash in town!"

"I ain't seen nuthin' like this since the water started changing colors." Frankie "The Tongue" Gambini was speaking on behalf of the Amphibians. The bullfrog's eyes were moist with emotion. "That first week alone we lost a dozen fish, three times that many frogs."

The rest of the Alliance murmured collectively at the memory of the awful catastrophe caused by the paper mill.

"But that was explainable." It was Fat Mama, hanging by a thread in the center of the meeting. As head of the entire Pond Alliance, she had to be cautious in situations like this. Panic would spread swiftly, and all the facts needed to be weighed carefully. "I'm sure the answers lay before us," she said. "If we can only ask the right questions."

In the center of the flat rock lay two stinking, rotten fish. A third was so disgusting that no one would carry it over from the weeds at the water's edge. Poor Pudge kept his distance from it all, and did his best to stay upwind. His stomach was still queasy from the morning's discovery.

Circling the carcasses was Dr. Kim Kym, a delicate, officious fruit bat who had been roused from her daytime sleep to examine the evidence.

"Hm. Curious abrasions . . . bloated eyes . . . no apparent scars . . ." Dr. Kym poked at the scaly bodies, looking closely at the rotting skin and making mental notes as she continued.

Dr. Kym, an expert in disease and death, hated working in the daytime and resented the Alliance for never having nocturnal meetings. Still, examining dead bodies was her job and she did it yawningly, with accuracy and skill.

"These two corpses fit the pattern of the earlier discoveries. Yet my findings are inconclusive. I'd say after a quick examination that the cause of death is suspicious."

A hushed whisper rose from the meeting. Fat Mama immediately clicked her legs for attention.

"Suspicious, Dr. Kym? Do you suspect foul play?"

The bat looked back at the fish sprawled before her. Something wasn't right, but she couldn't put her wing on it. "I am a scientist; I don't make conjectures. I assess facts, and the facts as I see them are: we have dead fish washing up on our shore. Dead fish whose demise is uncertain."

"But last time—da humans killed da water. And da water killed us!" Flakes had spoken aloud the very same thought that everyone else had: *Are the humans doing it again?*

Dr. Kym eyed the crowd. She was aware of how much they depended on her scientific point of view. She knew she couldn't tell them that she too was worried that the dead fish might be a sign that the Pond was again becoming unlivable. But that was just a feeling, not a fact. And it was up to the facts to tell the whole story.

"I can't say whether the humans are behind this or

not," the bat said. "Now, if you'll excuse me, I have a date with a tree branch. Good night."

"I say it's all because of the humans." The General's voice whispered to the one-eyed skunk by his side. "I, for one, am sick and tired of having to live with their poison."

"I hear ya loud and clear," responded Hinky. The skunk raised his voice, hoping to incite the crowd. "The people are doin' it! I say we put them in their places!"

Everyone knew that Hinky was a hysterical human-hater, but maybe this time he was right. Several mammals voiced agreement. A horde of bees buzzed excitedly. Toads and frogs voted with off-key croaks.

Fat Mama tried to regain order to the meeting, but the snowball of dissent was building and gaining momentum.

The General smiled to himself. One talon at a time, claw by claw, step by slow step. His plan to overthrow the Alliance was taking shape.

Who would've known that rotten fruit, the kind covered with pus-like bruises and swarming fruit flies, tasted so delicious? Oliver the boy would've been disgusted, but Oliver the crow was happily devouring the rancid treat, down to the seeds and pits.

Antoine was just happy to be back at the dump with the garbage crew. This mishmash of castoffs was Antoine's only real family among the crows. It felt good to be home again.

"This is a particularly flavorful delicacy we like to call 'mangled meat.'" His old pal Reggie was acting as waiter, maitre d', and busboy for Antoine and the ravenous Oliver.

The older crow placed a hunk of something disgusting in front of the two, and it was first come, first served as they fought over the pickings.

"You lookin' skinny as ever, 'Toine!" Reggie had called out when he'd first seen the two crows land among the broken toilets and discarded car parts. He then shot a curious glance at Oliver, who still looked slightly nauseated, and added, "And what's with your buddy? He's actin' like he never seen good eatin'."

But that was hours ago, and Oliver had gotten used to the smell of the place as quickly as he swallowed his first bite of what might have been the same rancid roast beef his mother had tossed out just three days earlier. How could he actually eat this? And how could it possibly taste so good? He didn't know and didn't care. He just dove in for more.

"And that squishy taste," offered Reggie as Oliver mulled over the new sensation in his mouth. "That's li'l maggots. Mmmmm. You're so lucky you came today. Tomorrow they'd be flies!"

As the sun set, the eating gave way to dancing and singing, and for the first time, Oliver realized that Antoine had a nice voice.

Maybe you have to be a crow to hear it this way, Oliver told himself as he joined in with the others, a chorus of cackling crow voices harmonizing with Antoine's solos.

Soon Oliver found himself dancing awkwardly as the outstretched wings of his new friends formed a circle around him. Without even trying, without ever worrying, Oliver was immediately accepted for who he was.

And who he was at that moment, at that garbage dump, in that body—was a scraggly, cackling, laughing, happy crow.

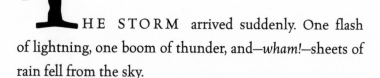

CHAPTER FIFTEEN

THE STORM arrived suddenly. One flash of lightning, one boom of thunder, and—*wham!*—sheets of rain fell from the sky.

The rain's staccato rhythm beat out an angry, sopping wet song on the old roof.

"Mo-*ther!*" Rachel's needs could always be measured by the tone she used when calling her mother's name, and this one immediately meant trouble.

"It's raining . . . *in my room!*"

Carol ran to the kitchen, grabbed two large pots, and

then raced up the stairs, two at a time. The first leak was easy, the second messy, but it was the third that surprised them both when a piece of soggy ceiling plopped down, followed by buckets of water that soaked their heads.

Rachel screamed. Carol laughed. And in the room next door, Mooch shuddered under the rock in his tank, wondering why that stupid crow hadn't brought Oliver back yet.

The storm caught Antoine and Oliver by surprise too. The garbage party had ended with a sticky dessert of mud-dipped melon rinds, and both crows were fat and happy on their flight back home.

The sudden shift of wind was all Antoine needed to revert to his teacherly ways. "And what does *that* tell you?" he asked, testing Oliver on what he'd been taught earlier in the day.

"Er, it's windy?" Oliver guessed.

But even before Antoine could lift a wing to jokingly smack him on the head, the rain hit. It was cold and, of course, wet—but worse than that—suddenly the crows found it almost impossible to navigate. The headwind forced Oliver to work hard at flying, to exert all his energy just to stay in the air. There was no gliding this time—just constant wing-flapping concentration.

Oliver suddenly rememberd a dreadful canoe trip he had been forced to go on, at a summer camp he had hated.

The morning had been great as he had floated lazily downstream with the other campers. The big clumsy paddles were used to splash each other and to steer away from the occasional rocks. But the afternoon's return trip was against the current, and the work to paddle back was excruciating. He was embarrassed to remember how he'd started to cry, and even the counselors had called him a wimp.

"Antoine, I can't do this!" he shouted. "My wings are killing me. I can't see. And I think my stomach is finally realizing that the junk food we ate really was *junk*."

Antoine was experienced at flying in the rain, but still he hated it too. He nodded toward the ground with his beak and yelled through the wind, "We'll wait it out down there."

In the spring and summer, the woods were a perfect place to stay dry in the rain. The thick leaf-covered branches made a canopy that kept even the biggest storms down to a drizzle. But in the fall, each downpour stripped the branches a little more, until the trees stood naked and raw.

Willy was waiting out the storm inside the dry hideout that he and Mooch had made at the base of the maple tree. So much had happened since the last time he had been there. Not only had his obsession with being a bigshot leader ruined his best friendship ever, he'd also lost the respect of the other insects. Willy knew they were sick of his whole "insect kids will make a difference" story and were all laughing behind his back. Lately, it was all starting to sound just as stupid to him too.

Antoine and Oliver were just a few feet away from Willy at that moment, huddled underneath the slight overhang of a rock that jutted out of a steep embankment near the thicket of oak and maple trees. The water flowed around the two crows in small rivers, and the first hints of a chill had settled in. As wet as they both were, they were happy to not be fighting the headwind, and secretly, Oliver was just glad to be back on solid ground.

"By the way, if I didn't say it earlier—um, thanks," Oliver said to Antoine.

"Hey, no need. Just seeing you enjoy yourself tonight was plenty of thanks for me, Ollie boy," said the crow.

He meant it too. He felt a little sad for the kid. Oliver didn't seem to have human friends, and didn't really do much of anything besides hang around with Mooch. Antoine sensed that, like himself, Oliver was a bit of an outcast.

Suddenly, a flash of lightning illuminated the woods. The thundering boom that followed only four seconds later was so huge it shook the ground and Oliver reached a wing toward Antoine.

"Lightning's really close by," he said nervously, just a breath ahead of the next flash. "I think we—" But Oliver's words were drowned out by a trembling explosion of thunder, which felt like it was directly above them.

"Ahhhhhh!" both crows shouted in terror, hugging each other tightly.

Willy felt the thunder shake his tree hideout and knew better than to stay inside the wooden fortress. There were plenty of other dry places to wait out the weather, and he flew out into the rainy night to find one.

He dodged the huge drops of rain and landed beneath a boulder, unaware of how close he was to the two soaking wet crows.

"Antoine, I hope you don't take this the wrong way, but I really want to get out of this body." Oliver was shivering now, and his friend could see how afraid and cold he was.

"No offense taken, kiddo. Besides, that's not a great body anyway. You really should work out—flabby wings are such a turnoff." Antoine was doing his best to make the boy laugh.

Oliver knew the drill. He just had to close his eyes and calmly wish his way back. But his heart was racing, and each time he came close to the dizzy feeling of return, his mind got in the way and feelings of fear roared back, making the transformation impossible.

"It's not working," Oliver shouted above another shock of thunder. "Something's wrong!"

Antoine saw the terror in Oliver's eyes.

"What if it doesn't work anymore? Maybe I used it all up. I don't want to be a stupid crow! WhatdoIdo? WhatdoIdo?"

"Is that someone yelling?" Willy asked himself, hearing the frantic voice drift in and out of the storm's disturbing sound track.

The dragonfly peered through the curtain of rain. At first all he could see was a blurry vision of trees and rocks, but then he spied them—the two crows huddled closely together. Willy recognized Antoine immediately and wondered what he was doing to the other crow.

Antoine was shaking Oliver. It was hard to tell if he was trying to chase the fear out of him or scare him even more. "Stop freaking out! You can't be such a mess! I need ya, okay, kid?"

"I . . . don't . . . know . . . what . . . to . . . do," Oliver said. "Just . . . stop . . . *shaking me!*"

Oliver was breathing hard. "I just have to let go of being scared."

"Great. Do that thing you do. Everything's gonna be okeydokey."

Oliver closed his eyes. Each breath became less frantic until finally he made the wish. His mind was blank and quiet. But just as the familiar swirling feelings began to overtake him—*flash! boom!*—a bolt of lightning sizzled just before a gut-rumbling burst of thunder. He had to calm down, so he shut his eyes tighter and forced the fear away. A moment later, there he was—a human boy sitting on the ground, soaked and cold, but ecstatic.

"We did it, Antoine! We did it!" Oliver hugged the little crow.

"No, buddy. YOU did it," Antoine said. "It was all you."

Willy was stunned. Did he really just watch a crow

turn into a boy? *That* boy? Mooch's kidnapper? And what was he doing with the foolish crow from the cage? What crazy stuff was Mooch mixed up in?

Willy's wings vibrated against the pelting rain. He was hovering above the wet rock, watching as the boy gathered the crow into the safety of his shirt and disappeared in the downpour.

"Get a grip, man," Willy told himself. He squinted through his wet gaze; the rain made the vanishing shapes even more blurry than the crazy memory of what had just happened.

But Willy was also not the only one who had witnessed the strange transformation. Someone else had seen it all too. Someone who would like nothing better than to use the incident to his own advantage.

CHAPTER SIXTEEN

IT WAS MONDAY morning and Oliver's fever had finally gone down. Saturday night had been the worst. His hacking cough and hundred and two temperature scared his mother enough to sit by his bed all day Sunday, nursing him with homemade soup and asking over and over why he hadn't had enough sense to come in from a storm like that. "And I still don't understand why you had that mangy crow wrapped inside your shirt."

She felt his forehead for the millionth time that morning. "Maybe this is a bad idea. . . ."

"I'll be fine, Mom," Oliver said in a nasal, tired voice.

"I'm old enough to be home alone. Besides, I have all your telephone numbers at school."

"I just hate to think you don't need me anymore," his mom replied, standing up. "Get lots of rest. There's a thermos of chicken soup on the counter. Call me for any reason. *Anything.*"

She bent down and kissed his forehead before disappearing out the door. For a split second Oliver did feel that staying home from school all alone wasn't a good idea. But then Antoine sneezed, reminding Oliver that he wouldn't be alone at all.

"Gesundheit, Antoine," Oliver said.

"Thanks, pal," the sniffly bird called back. "Man, I hate having a cold."

Oliver blew his nose and tossed the wet tissue onto the growing mountain that lay on the floor. He was dead tired from his adventure with Antoine. His shoulders were stiff and his arms still had the lingering feeling of being wings. Looking across the room, he saw that Mooch was fast asleep, which looked appealing, Oliver slid out of his bed and shuffled to the cage, scooping the salamander into his hand.

"Come on, buddy. Snooze with me," Oliver said as he climbed back into bed. He placed the snoring Mooch on his pillow, then rolled over and closed his eyes, sliding into the dizzy dreamy place where he was still flying high above the world.

Downstairs, Rachel was almost out the door when she stopped short, screaming, "I forgot to put on my striped socks!"

"Honestly, Rachel, can we be on time just once before they fire me?" Carol asked impatiently, jiggling the car keys.

"Mother. My ensemble is wrecked without the proper accent. I bought those socks to go with these new shoes!"

Carol shook her head as Rachel raced back upstairs. "Just don't wake your brother," she called.

Rachel ransacked her room, tore apart the laundry basket in the hallway, and as a last resort, tiptoed into Oliver's room. Occasionally a stray article of her clothing got mixed in with his.

Oliver was already snoring. Rachel walked quietly to his dresser and opened the top drawer.

She rummaged through the sea of white cotton. Tube socks. Crew socks. Sports socks. She was just about to give up when her hand brushed against something hard and glassy. She pulled out Oliver's secret gem by its leather string.

"Whoaaa," she said, admiring its golden color. She held it up against her green sweater and smiled. "Good-bye, striped socks; hello, necklace." She slipped the gem around her neck and ran back downstairs.

As Rachel rode with her mother to school, it never occurred to her that she had opened a door she'd never be able to close again.

All she knew was: the necklace made her hair look great.

The General was pacing on the rock. Below him, the skunk was retelling his incredible story.

"It's like I said, I was waiting out the storm and I seen it. *Bammo!* A crow turned into a kid. I saw it. It happened."

"Your one eye needs adjusting," snapped The General. "Crows don't turn into boys. Crows *hurt* boys!"

The General dragged a claw against the face of the rock. Hinky flinched.

"Yeah. Right. Whatever. All I'm saying is, I saw what I saw. And I thought you'd want to know." Hinky started to leave. He was finished with this conversation. The General was not.

"And why would I want to know?" the crow asked as he hopped down, blocking Hinky's exit.

"Because," Hinky answered cautiously, "your nephew was with him."

The General remembered the two crows he'd seen the day before. One was his silly nephew but the other was oddly out of place. Maybe, no matter how absurd it sounded, this skunk was telling the truth.

"Perhaps I'm not being fair." The General smiled at Hinky, who wasn't sure what to make of the crow's sudden change of mood.

"Please," The General said warmly, "come and join me for a bite. We have much to discuss."

Hinky swallowed hard. There was something menacing in The General's tone, and Hinky liked it a lot.

Sixth period was Rachel's biology class. Walking into the smelly classroom, she recoiled a bit. Sure, Little Falls High wasn't known for its cutting-edge fashion sense, but it seemed the entire class was dressed in the ugliest outfits she'd ever seen.

Everyone was wearing unflattering pants. And all the shoes were style-neutering rain boots or those "duck shoes" she detested—a work boot top on a molded rubber sole. The bell rang and Ms. Forsythe entered, wearing the most ridiculous outfit of all: waist-high rubber overalls, rain boots, and a pith helmet. She also carried a long net, which made her look more cartoonish than usual.

Rachel had just taken her seat when it hit her. "Up and at 'em, Miss Durkin. It's field trip time!"

Of course! Today was the day she'd meant to stay home sick because they were supposed to go outside to the small soggy pond behind the school to catch frogs. *Frogs!* She had forgotten about it, and consequently not worn frog-catching clothes. Rachel was not a fan of slimy or smelly, and was even less in favor of spending an hour ruining her new ninety-dollar shoes.

"Um, Ms. Forsythe, I don't feel so good." Rachel put on

her best pathetic face. "Maybe I should just sit in the library instead."

Ms. Forsthye put her hand on Rachel's shoulder. Instead of a soothing pat, it was an iron grip.

"Every year someone tries to weasel out of capturing the frogs that we dissect. And every year I tell them the same thing: catching the frog is fifty percent of the grade. Cutting it open is thirty percent."

"But what's the other twenty percent?" Rachel asked, unsure she wanted to know the answer.

Ms. Forsythe leaned close and sneered. "You get the last twenty percent of the grade for not making me mad."

The class walked from the main building and across the parking lot, looking like an oddball safari. Rachel was with Pam Dinsmore, a girl who'd had the good sense to ditch her usual bright palette for khaki and olive.

"I hear she makes us name the frogs so that when we have to dissect them it flips us out. She's wacko."

Rachel hated to imagine the "dissection" part of the assignment. Just the thought of having to cut open and then dig around a frog's belly to locate a miniscule large intestine or pea-sized kidney nearly made her puke.

"Step lively, class. I don't tolerate stragglers," Ms. Forsythe shouted. "We don't want to disappoint the froggies."

Rachel noticed her mother's car parked a few feet away and, seeing the back window open, had a fleeting thought of escape. But knowing that Ms. Forsythe had an eye on her, she thought better of it and just kept trudging on; past the grassy football field, past the deafening lawn mowing tractor, and over to the algae-infested pond behind the school, known to the kids as "Pus Puddle."

"Remember, eyes open. Hands alert. Destiny will match you to your croak-mate." Ms. Forsythe was already up to her armpits in the muck, and Rachel had to agree with Pam's earlier assessment: she was wacko.

Mooch crawled over Oliver as he lay in bed. "Come on, get up, Ollie. I'm hungry."

Oliver raised his knees under the blankets, making Mooch seemingly rise to the top of a mountain peak. "I'm sick, Mooch. I gotta stay in bed." He blew his nose. "I prom- ise I'll get up soon. Bed just feels so nice."

"For you! Sure." Mooch sank down on the soft blanket. He was angry and pouty. Mooch looked over at Antoine. "It's all *his* fault."

"Me? Now, don't get your tail in a knot, Plumpso! It's just a little biddy cold."

"Yeah? Well, *why's* he got a cold, huh? I didn't keep him out in the storm, did I? No-o-o-o. It was you, Featherhead!"

"*Featherhead?!*" After years of verbal abuse from his uncle, Antoine hated being called names. He fired back. "I'll say this slowly so's maybe you can understand me. Maybe, just maybe, Oliver prefers the wings of flight to the web toes of YOU!"

"Yeah, right. Like he'd really prefer being a crow! That's a good one."

Antoine stuck his beak between the bars of his cage. "The food chain speaks for itself, kiddo. Last time I checked, *you* were on my breakfast menu!"

Oliver had had enough. He tried jumping in. "Um, guys—"

"Shut up!" Antoine and Mooch shouted, as they continued the fight that would clearly have no winner.

Rachel had carefully taken off her new shoes and left them on the grass before rolling up her pants and stepping into the water.

So much for painting my toenails, she thought as she watched her bright red nails sink into the brown silt.

Standing off from the other kids with her feet submerged in the thick mud, she watched as her classmates stalked their prey with mixed results. This would never be happening if she still lived in the city. There were no ponds. No frogs. No gooey mud that ruined pedicures.

"Here, froggie, froggie, froggie!"

Rachel turned and saw Brody Shrank, the thick-necked son of the real estate agent whom Rachel still blamed for finding them a home. He was splashing around, scaring the frogs and meeker classmates with his obnoxious laugh.

"Ten more minutes!" Ms. Forsythe called out from her

waist-deep stance in the pond. "And anyone without a frog loses fifty percent of their grade!"

Enough already with the frogs, Rachel thought as she took another cautious step into the muck. She was determined to get this over with as quickly as possible, and was immediately rewarded with the sight of two bulbous eyes watching her from the water.

She'd seen Oliver do this enough times to know she had to be fast and certain. Even though she dreaded touching the icky thing, she dreaded Ms. Forsythe even more.

Rachel scooped her hand into the water, grabbing the fat frog's body. She couldn't believe she'd actually done it, and almost shouted out, caught up in the excitement of the moment.

As she lifted the frog from the water the sun broke through a cloud. Instantly, the gem dangling from her neck caught the sunshine, and the golden color inside seemed to glow. She'd forgotten about the necklace and wished she'd taken it off so it wouldn't get wet.

Rachel couldn't help but admire the way the gem caught the light. In fact she was so surprised at the glowing stone that she loosened her grip slightly. Sensing the shift, the frog seized the moment and jumped.

If only he'd jumped back into the water or over her head. But the frog was also curious about the golden shining thing, and jumped straight at Rachel.

"Eowww, gross," were the last words she spoke as a girl.

The next thing Rachel knew, she was sitting in the water.

"Sorry about that," said a deep voice next to her. Totally disoriented, she turned her head and saw that she was sitting in the mud next to the frog she'd just caught. But if that were true, she'd have to be his size. And—wait a second—frogs don't talk!

A second later she caught her own reflection in the water and nearly passed out. She was a frog.

Before she even had time to freak out, a muddy boot splashed down next to her. Rachel was still too stunned to move.

"Gotcha!" a booming voice called out.

She looked up as Brody Shrank's giant hand dropped out of nowhere, grabbing her.

"Yo! I got mine," he shouted to his buddies Meatball and Fred, who were still empty-handed.

Brody held Rachel tightly, pumping his prize like it was one of those rubber toys whose eyes bulge with each squeeze. Then he traced a line down her pale bumpy belly.

"The first slice goes right here. I can't wait."

Rachel screamed as loud as she could, but it came out as a sickening *croak*. She prayed she was dreaming, but knew she wasn't. She also knew she didn't want to be a frog. She didn't want to be cut open. And she certainly didn't want to be touched by stupid Brody Shrank.

The school bell rang in the distance. Ms. Forsythe

waved her net in the air. "Time's up! Anyone with a frog now gets extra credit. Anyone without comes back after school. No frog—no grade."

The kids began the slow trek back to the building. Those with frogs would label theirs and place them inside a large glass jar—which would then be filled with formaldehyde-soaked cotton balls. The fumes would overtake the frogs slowly, and by morning they'd all be lifeless specimens, cadavers to be dissected, all in the name of science.

"Dead frog walking!" Brody called out as he carried Rachel high above his head. Meatball laughed. Fred, as usual, didn't get it.

Rachel was frantic. She didn't have time for the *hows*, *whats*, or *whys* of her current situation. She had to think, and she had to think fast.

They were halfway across the playing field when the idea came to her. Brody still held her high in the air, playing with her as if she were some sort of action toy.

"It's a bird. It's a plane. It's a frog!"

Rachel shut her eyes tight and did what any girl trapped inside the body of a frog would do. She peed.

Brody felt the liquid flood his hand, then drip onto his head. He dropped the frog in disgust and Rachel knew this was her only chance for escape.

She had never been much of a runner, but she'd never been a frog before either. She used her new powerful legs to shoot five feet at a time, away from Ms. Forsythe's class.

"Dude, your frog," said Meatball.

"Forget the frog," replied Brody, wiping his hand on Fred. "It took a whiz on me."

Rachel leaped toward the safety of the tall grass at the far end of the field. She felt her tiny heart pumping wildly, and for a split second, imagined her own frog insides, all those miniature organs, as if she'd dissected herself in her mind.

After five minutes in the uncut grass, she felt safe. The class had gone back inside, and now she was left to figure out what to do next. Everything looked so far away. She felt small and frightened—and fat! Tears came to her eyes and she sobbed in deep belching breaths.

All at once the earth began to shake. She felt the rumbling vibrations of what seemed like an earthquake.

As the ground tremors continued, her tiny ears filled with a deafening sound that froze her on the spot. She looked left—then right—but she was so small and hidden that all she saw were the towering blades of grass and endless dirt.

The noise got louder and the ground shook more ferociously. She needed to see above her grassy hiding spot, so she began to jump straight up, each time looking in a different direction. Facing forward, she saw the football squad entering the field for practice. She jumped up again, this time facing left, and saw the edge of the awful pond. Facing right was the school parking lot. She leaped into the air one final time, and there it was—coming straight at her—a massive lawn mowing tractor.

She landed in the grass and didn't waste a single moment. She leaped wildly one or two feet ahead of the sharp blades that whirred fiercely on either side of the tractor, chomping the grass into freshly chewed mulch. Either the heavy tractor would run her over or she'd be shredded into a frog smoothie; neither choice appealed to a girl who had yet to be kissed.

Jump. Land. Jump. Land. Rachel's choices were limited by her current body's natural ability. She tried to jump just a little farther each time but soon found that this exhausted her. The mower was gaining.

She felt the heat from the blades on her back and she accepted that this was it: she was about to be sliced and diced. She had to laugh because her fate seemed sealed. She was either going to be dissected by a student or a machine. How ironic and disgusting was that?

Still, Rachel kept jumping—she wouldn't give up that easily. And just when she was certain she was about to die, the tractor veered left, and she realized she had jumped clear of the tall grass and onto the smooth surface of the playing field.

"I did it. I'm alive!" she shrieked, then remembered in what form she was alive.

She carefully made her way across the football field, dodging the sharp cleats of the players who sprinted above her.

Rachel finally jumped onto the warm tar of the parking lot and hopped around, looking for her mother's car. She had to find it before her mom drove off. She had to get home.

At her normal height it would've taken about a minute to spot the car. But from her new vantage point on the ground it wasn't so easy. A skateboarding classmate nearly rolled over her, and a cheerleader in a pink convertible nearly flattened her. But finally she saw the red battered car. Rachel hopped through the open back window and hid on the cool floor, feeling safer, and yet more afraid than she'd ever felt before.

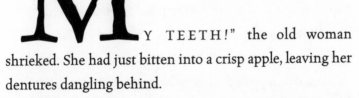

CHAPTER SEVENTEEN

"**M**Y TEETH!" the old woman shrieked. She had just bitten into a crisp apple, leaving her dentures dangling behind.

"Humans are so poorly built," Antoine said, disgusted as the woman on the television squirted thick goo on her false teeth before popping them back into her concave mouth.

Oliver, Mooch, and Antoine were lying together on the bed watching TV. Oliver had dug out his old television as a final solution for shutting up the salamander and crow, who'd spent the whole morning yelling at each other.

Back in the city, Oliver used to watch so much TV, he knew what was on no matter what day or time it was. But as he dusted off the small television and hooked it up to the makeshift antenna on the roof, Oliver realized he hadn't watched the tube since he'd found the gem. Ironically, he had found the gem because he wanted to watch TV so bad he'd gone up on the roof—and been chased by a crazy crow who now sat next to him in bed, sipping hot soup. Weird.

Mooch and Antoine were mesmerized by the images that flashed in front of them. Trapped in that little box, people spun huge colorful wheels and won cars, held each other tightly and kissed, ate chewy chocolaty candies that made Mooch's mouth water. In fact, more than once, Oliver had to stop the salamander from licking the screen.

"But it looks so good," Mooch pleaded. He became angry when a commercial ended and the candy (or cookies, or pizza) disappeared, only to be replaced by images of toilet paper or tile cleaner. Antoine, of course, was less discriminating, and decided he could devour almost everything he saw.

Despite their differences, the two creatures agreed on one thing: it sure looked like fun being a kid. According to the TV, kids lived fast-paced, batteries-not-included lives, and ate snacks, played video games, and flirted all day.

"Hello? It's just the dumb commercials. Advertising isn't real," Oliver insisted.

But Mooch and Antoine were too busy wishing that they were the ones eating rolled-up fruit leathers or rushing down city streets on tiny wheels attached to their shoes.

Oliver couldn't help but laugh. In one short afternoon, he had hooked his two friends on the one thing he no longer needed.

The General flew as high as he could, with the conviction that he was more powerful than any of the other pond scum beneath him. He felt more and more that his destiny was coming closer. He was rising to his position, the position he should have always had. The head of the Pond Alliance.

Crows are smarter, stronger, more adaptable, he thought. This was his mantra.

"I will take over," he always said to himself—even as he smiled dutifully at Fat Mama, obeying her insipid orders to keep peace among the Pond species. Oh, how he longed to squash her. To slowly pluck her legs off and watch her writhe in pain before she withered away.

When the Alliance voted her into power, he was outraged. A spider? Over a crow? He knew he could easily overthrow her, make a meal of her entire brood. But he was smart. Cunning. He knew to truly rule he would need one thing more than anything else. FEAR.

He had carefully formed a plan. A plan that used fear to infect the entire Pond. Just as it had been the catalyst for forming The Alliance, *fear* would dissolve it. *Fear* would make the other creatures question their leadership. *Fear* would squish the spider just as easily as if he'd stepped on her himself. And at the height of the tension and turmoil, when the fear, had penetrated them all—HE would step up to the plate and provide the antidote. He would become their leader—because *they* wanted it. And they would be thankful to him and would never even know he had orchestrated the whole thing.

But that was his original plan. The plan he'd made before finding out about the boy becoming a crow. He turned the image over and over in his mind, knowing that whatever strange power the boy had would fit perfectly into his new takeover plans.

All he had to do was wait.

"Just once I wish she'd think of someone other than herself." Crouched in the backseat, Rachel heard her mother's voice outside the car and could tell how furious she was.

"Well, tomorrow she'll be here on time if she wants a ride home." Carol opened the car door and got inside. She tossed her heavy bag into the backseat, unaware of how close she had come to squashing her only daughter.

Rachel stayed quiet. She wanted to scream out for help

but was afraid if her mother realized a frog was in the car, she would just toss it back outside. Rachel needed to get home. To jump into bed, close her eyes, and dream herself away from this nightmare.

Oliver heard his mother's car rattling down the dirt road during an episode of *Grillin' with Grady*, a cooking show that Mooch insisted they watch.

Grady, a silver-haired good ol' boy with a belly that stuck out like an extra person, was adding freshly ground pepper to a flank steak as it sizzled over mesquite wood coals. "And ya gotta sear both sides brown or the juice will run loose like a diaperless baby."

Oliver switched off the set.

"Hey!" yelled Mooch and Antoine in stereo. "We're watching that."

But Oliver wanted his mother to think he'd rested all day, and quickly put the TV into the closet. Then he returned Mooch and Antoine to their respective cages.

"I'm gonna pretend I'm sleeping. No noise. Got it?"

They got it. Even though they didn't like it.

"One thing though," Mooch insisted hungrily. "When do I get a grilled steak? Huh? When?"

"Rollerblades for me!" shouted Antoine as he rattled the cage with his beak. "And a girlfriend!"

Oliver sank into his bed and pulled the covers over his head. "I hate TV," he moaned.

Inside the car Rachel acted fast. She knew she had one

chance to get from the backseat and into the house unnoticed. She leaped into her mother's schoolbag just as the back door swung open. Rachel found herself squished between a steel coffee thermos and a massive chemistry textbook. She held her breath, hoping she wouldn't croak involuntarily and spoil her free ride.

Inside the house, her mom dropped the bag at the bottom of the stairs, and Rachel felt the weight of the huge chemistry book shift, suddenly trapping her left foot. (Foot? Flipper? *Whatever!*) As soon as her mother walked away, Rachel frantically wriggled free.

Slowly, Rachel raised her head over the edge of the bag. The coast was clear. She wasn't sure what to do, but she knew she had to get upstairs. And with no one else to turn to she realized her weirdo brother was probably her best hope. She took a deep breath and, with one strong push of her legs, jumped free of the bag. All she needed to do now was conquer the stairs and begin her journey back to being a girl.

When Oliver heard his door creak open he quickly put his head on the pillow and closed his eyes. He hoped his mother would check in, then check out. Adios.

After a moment of soft fake snoring, he peeked out of his left eye and was relieved to see no one was there. He relaxed, stretching under the warm covers, and thought maybe a real nap would be nice. It had been a pretty tiring day dealing with Mooch and Antoine.

Suddenly Oliver felt something fall on his bed.

He sat up and looked around but still didn't see anything. Until it jumped again and landed on his chest.

"Ahh! A frog!" he shouted, more out of surprise than fright. What the heck was a frog doing in his room?

Oliver reached down and lifted the thing up to his face. Something about the creature looked so familiar. Maybe it was one of the pond creatures he'd met on an outing with Mooch. Yes, that must be it.

"I'm sorry," Oliver said. "I've forgotten your name."

The frog blinked and then finally opened its mouth. "I'm Rachel, you dimwit! *Rachel!*"

Oliver nearly fainted.

"Rachel? My sister, Rachel?"

The frog nodded.

"Oh, no, it's the loudmouthed shrew!" shouted Antoine. "Attack it before she yells again!"

Rachel whipped around. "Okay, crow, I've had about enough of your shouting and screeching and . . ." She hesitated. ". . . *Talking?*"

"I bite too!" he said, snapping his beak sharply in her direction.

Mooch shook his head. "Don't mind him. He's highstrung. We just ignore him."

Rachel looked at Mooch, then back at grinning Antoine. She didn't say a thing. She was shocked.

"It's okay, Rachel. It's all okay. I can understand them too. You're not crazy."

"Oh, that's good," she croaked. "Because for a moment there I *thought* I *was a frog!*"

The tears flowed from her protruding eyes. Oliver gently stroked his big sister's bumpy back, trying to calm her down. He'd never been the bigger one, and the role reversal felt oddly nice.

Oliver got Rachel to recount the whole dreadful day. He guessed she had somehow gotten a hold of the gem, but wanted to hear the story anyway. Truthfully, there was a small part of him that wanted to delay her return. He wanted to let her stay a frog a little longer, enjoying the power shift in their relationship that would vanish as soon as she changed back.

Rachel felt ridiculous hearing that all she had to do was calmly wish her way back. "Like, duh. How many dumb kid movies have I seen?"

Still, she was glad it was easy. Glad there would be no "eye of newt" potions. Glad that her little brother was there.

Oliver placed her on the floor. Together with Mooch and Antoine, he watched as the frog became a bright light that swirled into his sister. Stunned, she inspected her hands and then her bare feet.

"My ninety-dollar shoes!" she shrieked.

Rachel was definitely back.

CHAPTER EIGHTEEN

PUDGE WAS FURIOUS. He and Hinky went back too far to keep anything from each other. Over the years they had become more like brothers than friends, which is why Pudge wanted to strangle the skunk, or knock him on the head with a dead fish—whichever would bring him back to his senses fastest.

"Hinky, you're being an absolute idiot!" Pudge said, slapping his paw at the yellow jackets, who were ruining their lunch of ripe fall blackberries and the crunchy carrotlike roots of Queen Anne's lace.

"Attack the humans? Again? That's his plan?"

"You have no idea what he's capable of, Pudge. He knows stuff. I trust him."

Pudge settled on a small branch, his wide girth spilling over each side. "The only thing The General can be trusted to do is stab you in the back. Open your eye, Hinky. He's trouble."

But Hinky's mind was made up. Humans had caused enough pain in his life, and ultimately his disgust for *them* was greater than his love for Pudge.

Back at the end of No-way Way, Oliver was thrilled to have someone he could confide in. But telling Rachel also meant sharing the secret, and that left him feeling like maybe he'd given up more than he was getting back.

There was also the slight problem of Antoine. Rachel was the oil to his water—and he was, frankly, just a pain in her butt.

Antoine called out to Oliver. "Don't you see what she's doing here? Ollie? Buddy? She's nudging you out, trying to take over your sweet deal."

Rachel walked over to the cage and peered in close. Antoine did everything he could not to bite her nose.

"Okay. One: I'm not trying to take anything from my brother. And two: maybe you forgot—but I can hear everything you say!"

Rachel turned away from the cage and held up the

stone, examining it closely. Just twenty-four hours ago she would've laughed at the thought that this translucent gem could transform a kid into another living creature. She was still a bit grossed out that she'd spent half a day as a frog, but the magical possibilities far outweighed the slimy memory.

"Amazing what one day can do to you, huh, Ollie?"

Oliver had to smile. Ever since the gem had entered his life, he was amazed at what *every* day could do.

"I dunno. Another dead fish washes up, and all she wants to do is 'wait 'n see'?" Flakes eyeballed the anxious faces around him. "Fat Mama sure seems calm about all dis. Maybe she's in on it. With da humans. It's just a feeling I got, but what if? Huh?"

Frankie slapped the mud with his back leg. "The only feeling you got is that chronic itch. Worried is one thing— but a conspiracy theory? You've taken too many knocks to the shell, Flakes!"

Away from prying eyes and whispered wings, five of the Six Family leaders were gathered under the cloak of a misty night, huddled by the edge of the Pond, holding a secret meeting to discuss what was on all of their minds.

The fat frog croaked before speaking again. "This ain't about the humans. It's about if she's strong enough to be in charge. Maybe it's time the spider took a nice long nap."

"Hello? Have you all lost your minds?" It was Pudge.

"We had enough confidence to vote Fat Mama into power. Now we just have to let her do her job."

No one spoke. The uncomfortable silence was filled by the lonely song of a distant loon.

"The trout agrees with our Amphibian friend," the dripping wet beaver said, translating the words of the Fish Elder, whose silver eyes were visible just below the murky Pond's surface. "Perhaps some changes should be made."

The General was being very careful not to tip his hand. He needed to look like a follower, even though he knew he was secretly pulling all of the strings. "My friends," he began softly, "the raccoon speaks wisely for once. Change isn't always a good thing. May I suggest our arachnid leader simply be given enough silk to hang herself?"

"Hanging's good," blurted the turtle. "Real good."

Pudge was disgusted, but the others agreed. Letting the spider make her own mistakes would be much easier than forcing her to step down. Or eating her. Or worse.

"Then we're in agreement," The General said, knowing full well that no one had the vaguest idea that what they'd really decided was to help destroy the Alliance.

CHAPTER NINETEEN

OLIVER WOULD always remember that week, and Rachel would spend the rest of her life trying to forget it.

Together, they used every trick they knew to stay home from school for the next four days. Soap in the eyes, hot water on the thermometer, and the last disgusting resort, pretending to vomit. Thankfully for them, their mom was too busy trying to stay on top of her teaching load to see through their various hoaxes. Each day she left them alone with a long list of "do's and don'ts," and lots of hot soup.

The first day, both kids were up as soon as the car disappeared down the dirt road. After a guilt-free breakfast of any sugar-coated cereal they wanted, Rachel spent the morning getting Oliver to download everything he knew about the strange gem. Where he found it, how he used it, what it felt like to fly. Question after question after question.

After her curiosity was satisfied, Oliver graciously let Rachel decide what creature they'd become first.

Rachel was excited about making her choice, but wanted to play it relatively safe. She wanted to make sure she had a happy, fun time: nothing poisonous, nothing that stung, nothing slimy, nothing that could give you warts. It took one hour and two banana-chocolate milk shakes, but finally the answer came to her.

"A rabbit," she excitedly announced. "We're going to be sweet, soft bunny rabbits."

"Rabbits?" Oliver tried to sound positive, but inside he was cringing. "Whatever you say, sis."

Mooch disappeared into the woods and found them a willing cottontail subject. Everything should've been wonderful. Rachel had held and hugged and even rubbed noses with countless bunnies at the pet store. They were the nicest, cutest, cuddliest animal she could imagine.

But holding something tame is very different from *being* something wild. And it didn't take long to watch a real rabbit family do real rabbit stuff for Rachel to pull her bunny brother aside and practically scream into his long ears.

"Get me out of here! They are the most disgusting, gross bunch of animals I have ever met, er, been . . . whatever!"

"What? You didn't know that rabbits are coprophagous?" Earlier that morning, Oliver had done a quick Internet search and was especially proud to remember the huge word, which meant rabbits were a species that actually ate their own waste pellets for nutrition.

Rachel thumped the ground with her large back foot. "There is, like, NO WAY I am eating my own . . . Eowww. I am so grossed out, I think I'm gonna . . ."

And she did. She hurled into a sneezeweed plant, ruining the rabbit family's lunch as she lost her own.

The second day home from school it was Oliver's pick: spiders! He just couldn't wait to experience firsthand what it was like to spin webs and sling silk like a superhero.

He'd done his research and learned that spider silk is actually a form of protein that shoots out in liquid from special glands, solidifying instantly. He'd found out that some spiders use their silk to help protect their eggs, some to catch prey. Ballooning spiders release strands of silk into the wind and then travel to wherever the thread lands. Cool.

Once again, Mooch gladly helped with the transformation project. After solemnly promising not to eat any of them, he gathered four spiders, each a different type of arachnid for Oliver to look over.

The house spider was too ordinary. The furrow spider too stuck-up (he'd insisted they call him by his Latin name, *Nuctenea cornuta*). And the pirate spider—"Argh, pick me, matey, and we'll dig for buried treasure!"—he was just too weird.

Finally Oliver made a decision. He and Rachel would become the exquisite lattice spider ("*Araneus Thaddeus*," the furrow spider corrected).

Oliver was drawn to the lattice spider's dark, orblike abdomen decorated in an explosion of yellow spots. But Rachel took one look, made her "ick" face, and simply changed the plan.

"I know I said 'okay' before, but—no way, José!" She grabbed the gem from her brother and used it to change herself into a beautiful, bright-breasted meadowlark.

Oliver was burning with anger. She totally did exactly what Antoine had warned. She'd taken over. He sat on the front steps watching Rachel's swirling flight around the Pond, praying that a hawk might be in need of a midday snack.

"Why didn't I just leave her as a frog?" he groaned to the little lattice spider, now dangling like a circus acrobat from his left pinky.

"I feel your pain, dude," the spider replied. "But I've got

fifty-eight brothers and sisters to deal with. Your family—your mess."

Rachel flew right over Oliver's head and shrieked, "Hey, Ollie, the yellow feathers really complement my eyes, don't you think?"

She was rubbing his face in it now. Oliver, forever the little brother, felt powerless and angrier than ever.

"Okay, okay. I'll go out on a limb for ya." It was the lattice spider, now climbing up Oliver's forearm. "Let's talk revenge."

A smile spread across Oliver's face as the spider whispered his plan. It was a little mean and a lot of fun, and if all went well, it would teach Rachel who was the boss.

The next day was warm and became almost hot as the sun baked the early October morning into a summery afternoon. Rachel and Oliver knew there wouldn't be too many of these toasty days left and emerged from the house in shorts and T-shirts.

"Okay, one more time: my gem, my rules." He clutched the jewel tightly in his hand. "Try and take it again, and I'll post those pictures of you as a bucktoothed six-year-old on the high school Web site."

Rachel had no choice but to agree. She knew her brother was capable of ruining her social status with the click of a mouse.

Oliver kicked off his shoes and socks and stepped into

the pond. Rachel hung back and screwed up her face in the same way she did when she was a little kid and had to eat spinach.

"I don't know. I'm not sure I can handle the frog-thing again."

"Not frogs. Fish. Pretty little fish." Oliver waded into the warm water, feeling powerful and suddenly sure of himself. "Bag out if you want to, but this could be the last swim of the year. And if you don't want to explore the deep with me, I'm more than happy to do it *alone*."

It took all of three seconds (Oliver was counting) before Rachel splashed into the shallow pond and pushed her way over to him.

"You think I'm gonna let you have any fun without me? Dream on."

Before using the gem, the two former city kids had seen the Pond as a swampy mosquito magnet. But at that moment, standing knee-deep and side-by-side, they saw a sparkling new world inviting them into adventure.

Perch and bass jumped hungrily to catch daredevil insects. Water strider bugs raced across the surface like speed skaters. Painted turtles basked on sun-soaked logs, periodically yelling "Geronimo!" as they pushed them-selves off into the cooling wet depths. And tiny whirligigs spun in dizzy tea-cup circles, their two pairs of compound eyes simultaneously watching what was going on both above and below the water.

"Remember how Mom wouldn't let you scuba dive last year when we were down in Florida?" Oliver was baiting her now as he took a step deeper.

"Yeah, like I'd really get hurt underwater *in a swimming pool!*" Rachel kept that event freshly marked on her Resentment Scorecard. "And the instructor was such a hottie."

"Well, let's see Mom stop you now." Oliver peered into the water, and in a flash, he grabbed a fish, the one Mooch had discreetly asked to help out in the spider's scheme to get back at Rachel.

Oliver held the gem in his free hand and pushed it toward Rachel. "Go ahead, grab on."

Rachel slid her fingers around the shiny surface. "This will be fun, right?" she asked, suddenly aware of a certain devilish look in her brother's eyes.

"Trust me. We're going to have more than just fun." Oliver smiled. Then he pulled his hand from the water, revealing a fat, whiskered, repulsive catfish. "Say hello to Mr. B."

Rachel's face barely had time to register disgust before—*splash!*—three catfish dropped into the sun-drenched water.

"Now, that kinda makes a crow's heart feel good," sighed Antoine, who had been watching Oliver's scheme unfold from the warm grass. "Turn the catty princess into a catty-fish. *Caaaawwwww!*"

Mooch didn't know exactly why, but he defended Rachel. "She may think only of herself, but she's not *all* bad, Antoine."

"Maybe you're right, Moochie. Maybe her little toe is good. But the rest—bad as it comes, my friend. Bad as it comes."

The catfish siblings sank deep below the surface through scattered rays of sunlight. Their murky surroundings came alive with different forms of algae, miniscule transparent water fleas and hydras, and hundreds of other moving, strange shapes that seemed to come straight out of a science fiction movie.

"You said I'd be a *pretty* fish!"

They were on the muddy bottom, and Rachel was staring at how wrinkled and yucky Oliver was. If she looked even remotely the same, she was appalled.

"Catfish *are* pretty. To other catfish." He was really enjoying this. "By the way, sis, your mustache is, like, so-o-o attractive."

That did it. She lunged for him, surprised at the ease of movement her fins provided. But Oliver was faster, and he darted off between the waving waterweeds and hornworts, carefully hiding behind an old winter boot that had sunk into the mud and now housed a family of Trapdoor snails.

Rachel stopped and yelled after him, "Come back here, or, or . . ."

"Or what?" a deep voice whispered nearby. She turned

around but didn't see anyone. The eerie voice continued. "Or you'll eat him? Like I want to eat *you?*"

She screamed, tiny air bubbles exploding upward from her wide whiskered lips. What she didn't know was that this was all part of the plan that Oliver, Mooch, and the lattice spider had set up.

"Who are you? *Where* are you?" Rachel trembled now, her fat lower lip quivering.

Oliver laughed as he watched the scene unfold.

Rachel was now stone still, her bulging eyes searching in all directions for the creature that wanted to have her for lunch. "Um, if it's all the same, I think I'll go now. B'bye."

Before she could bolt, her tormentor emerged from out of nowhere and grabbed hold of her fin with his strong jaws.

"Simon says, stop!" the voice mumbled through its clenched teeth. "Simon says, I'm gonna eat you whole!"

Simon was a Stinkpot turtle, who had been camouflaged as an algae-covered rock. He'd known Mooch since the amphibian was just a larva, so Simon had gladly agreed to the little charade.

"Please, don't eat me. I'm sure I taste really bad, and I have, like, a ton of homework to do and . . . and . . . HELP!"

Oliver was so amused by his sister's panic attack that he hardly noticed he had gotten snarled in the waterweeds and roots around him. He also didn't see that he had made some new friends, friends his mother probably wouldn't like—the kind who wanted to suck the life out of him!

The first pinch of pain on Oliver's back was immediately followed by two others. Swiveling his wide head around, Oliver saw that three thick brownish-green freshwater leeches had attached themselves to his scaly body.

"Thank you for donating blood to the Chug-a-lug Club." It was a fourth leech, floating a careful distance from Oliver's mouth. "I'm sure you know the drill, but just in case . . ."

The leech curled itself into a U shape and opened its front and rear sucker mouths wide, revealing two sets of sharp teeth. The two mouths spoke simultaneously, one in a female voice, the other male.

"One: our saliva is an antiseptic to numb the pain of our bite. Two: the same saliva keeps your blood thin, which makes it way easier for us to suck it out. And three: *resistance is futile!*"

The leech then attached its suckers onto Oliver's forehead, pushed its jaws open, and began to satisfy its thirst. The other leeches took a quick break and chanted in unison, "Open the jaws, bite and suck. Sorry, chum, you're out of luck! Chug-a lug!"

After a second or two of shock, Oliver shook himself like a wet dog, but the leeches weren't going anywhere—they just dug in deeper and sucked harder.

As he tried to flee, he realized in a panic that he was

too tangled in the weeds to escape. And now a half dozen new leeches joined the party, fighting over feeding spots and making Oliver weaker by the second.

And just when he thought things couldn't get any worse, a large shape descended through the thick water, like an alien mothership looking to land.

"Oh, man, you are one dead cat," said the leech closest to his face. "That's a giant water bug. Wait till you feel her poison turn your insides into mush before sucking them out like a cool drink! Hoo-boy, it is par-tay time!"

Oliver felt stupid and sick. He was in way over his head.

"Come on, it was just a little joke." Simon, the Stinkpot turtle, was trying to explain things to Rachel, who had finally stopped crying. "Sure, maybe my 'swallow you whole' speech was a tad over the top, but come on, all in the name of fun, right?"

He then confessed the whole thing was her brother's idea, which only fueled her anger.

"Hope this won't get in the way of our relationship." Simon was pouting. "You think I can see you again?"

"Yeah," Rachel said sarcastically. "See you real soon, *maybe in some soup.*"

For Rachel, that was it. Game over. She had had ENOUGH. All she wanted was to get out of that body, out of that pond, and to never talk to Oliver again.

"Um, Rachel—a little help here." She was swimming

quickly past Oliver, and even he knew it was a fruitless request on his part. At that moment she couldn't have cared less that he was fast food for the leeches, or that a water beetle was about to make him into a catfish smoothie.

"Help yourself!" she shouted back as she wiggled up toward the bright surface, where her life as a normal teenage girl waited.

Antoine wanted to laugh as the muddy, sopping-wet girl emerged from the water. But one look at her dark hateful eyes told him he'd live a longer, feathered life if he kept his trap shut.

Meanwhile, under the water, Oliver watched the water bug assassin lower herself closer, getting ready to inject him with the poison that would turn his catfish organs into soup. He should have been more frightened, but all those leeches and their blood-sucking, pain-killing saliva had made him woozy.

I wish I'd never done this, he thought, in the growing fog inside his head. "I wish I was me."

Like the sudden flush of a toilet, an unexpected rush overtook him. He hadn't even thought of trying to save himself by wishing he were a kid again. It just sort of happened and caught him totally off guard. Suddenly the pond bubbled and churned as Oliver the boy struggled weakly to the surface. As a fish he was near death, but as a much larger human he still had plenty of blood to go around and was merely dazed by the toxins in his body.

He was also still covered with the leeches.

"Leech! Leech!" Mooch saw them first and began screaming.

Rachel was almost inside the house when she heard Mooch cry out. Seeing her wet little brother and the slimy thick leeches stuck all over his body, she pushed her anger aside. She ran in to the house, got the first-aid kit, and did what she did best: she took charge.

"Don't pull them off. Their jaws can get stuck in your skin and that'll cause an infection." Rachel then turned to the shocked crow and salamander. "What? Three years in the Girl Scouts wasn't just to sell the stupid cookies."

She heated up the head of a safety pin with a match and touched each leech with the searing hot tip. She wielded the pin like a Jedi's lightsaber, and in a minute or two, Oliver was leech-less, but covered with strange bite marks as reminders of his ordeal.

"Thanks," he said sheepishly as Rachel dabbed each wound with antiseptic. He couldn't look her in the eyes.

"I never, ever, *ever* want to see this stupid thing again." She grabbed the gem from his neck and waved it at him. "And if I were you, I'd be very careful. It's trouble, Oliver. You shouldn't be messing with it."

She closed the first-aid kit, stood up, and walked briskly back toward the house. Oliver couldn't help but feel lousy for the way things had turned out. He wanted to run to Rachel and hug her, but that seemed impossible. He'd blown it—big time.

But suddenly Rachel stopped. Maybe she was feeling the same. Maybe he could make everything okay.

"By the way." Rachel lifted her arm. The sunlight caught something shiny, and Oliver remembered she was still holding the gem. "Say good-bye to your rock!"

She threw like a girl—a girl who'd been on a softball team for two summers. The gem twirled in a sparkling arc toward the Pond.

Mooch and Antoine held their breath as they watched Oliver try desperately to catch the golden pass before it disappeared in the water.

It all seemed to happen in slow motion: Oliver stumbled backward, then jumped. His arm extended, and amazingly, Oliver caught the gem. But as he fell, it bounced out of his hand and landed with a crack onto the pebbly shore.

"You broke it!" He immediately saw that a teardrop-shaped corner had chipped off. He was devastated. "Maybe it won't ever work again," he shouted at his sister. "I hate you!"

"Serves you right," was all Rachel said in reply, and she disappeared into the house.

Oliver spent the rest of the afternoon looking for the golden chip, to no avail. He finally went inside to drown his sorrow by watching game shows. Mooch and Antoine gladly followed.

For the next several hours the siblings avoided each other behind closed bedroom doors. Their mother finally came home from school, made dinner, and then sat at the kitchen table watching Oliver and Rachel pick at their plates in silence.

"Well, I'm glad to see things are back to normal around here," she said to the two, who wouldn't even make eye contact.

Oliver felt defeated and finally just went to sleep. But Rachel, slipped out late that night, hoping to find the broken shard of crystal.

"You never know," she said, as the flashlight beam finally bounced off the small piece of golden gem hidden under some weeds. "You just never know."

CHAPTER TWENTY

HE BONDING EXPERIENCE over
the gem had come and gone, and now Oliver and Rachel
had settled back into the comfort of their usual distance.
After the incident in the Pond, both were eager to get
back to school, neither wanting to discuss what had
happened.

"You have no idea what I've been through, Cherise."
Oliver was crouched just outside Rachel's room, straining
to hear everything she was saying on the phone. He hoped
for once that she'd be able to keep her big mouth shut and

not blow their secret. "I am just so glad you're coming up tomorrow. I have *so* much to tell you."

As if the week hadn't been long enough, now Oliver was dreading the weekend too. What bothered him most wasn't that his sister's best friend was coming for a visit, it was *how* Cherise was getting from the city to their house.

"By the way, you gonna be okay driving up here with my dad?" Rachel asked. "I mean, don't feel bad about tuning him out. That's what I do."

Oliver didn't stick around for any more of the phone call.

A few days ago, his father had sent him an e-mail. He was making the trip to Little Falls to tour some new building his company, BioProthesis Inc., had bought nearby. They'd taken over some closed-down paper factory and turned it into a "state-of-the-art" facility.

"It's just so typical," Oliver complained as he read the e-mail again. "Of course he's making the effort to see us. It's *convenient.*"

"Hey, crow-boy, what worm's eatin' you?" quipped Antoine, a clump of moldy cheese sticking out from his beak.

"My father. You wouldn't understand."

Antoine spit out the last bite of Limburger. "Wouldn't understand? Pal, my family's so dysfunctional, I prefer living in a *cage* to living with them!"

Mooch peered over the lip of his tank. "Back off. I think Oliver needs some space. You have heard of that, haven't you?"

Antoine eyed the salamander, searching for a snappy put-down. But he knew Mooch was right and silently went back to his cheese.

Oliver stared at the computer screen. He read about the updated progress of a thing his dad's company was working on, called "Project Fly-eye." Though he hated to admit it, the experiment actually sounded kind of cool. Using tiny cameras and an infrared transmission device, BioProthesis had built some sort of softball-sized fly eye and was experimenting to see whether they could re-create multi-lensed sight. According to the e-mail, that was just one of many experiments BioProthesis was doing in an attempt to get the jump on "the future of artificially enhanced body parts."

Reading this stuff, Oliver now almost looked forward to his father's visit. He knew all about what a fly's eyesight was like. They'd actually have some interesting things to talk about. But then he read the last sentence; the sentence his father had added to the e-mail. "Son, just a reminder how much I want to meet your friends. I'd hate to think you didn't have any! (Ha-ha! Just kidding—right?) See you Friday night. Dad."

And then Oliver hit DELETE.

* * *

As planned, his father had driven up from the city, dropped Cherise off at the house, gone off to tour the new work site, then picked the kids up to take them out for a late supper.

"Come on, gang. Dinner on the ol' man. Yes, sir. That's right. Are we gonna get this one-horse town to show us a good time, or what?" Arthur was in hyper-dad drive, and no one knew how to turn him off.

He was also on one of his desperate "divorced dad" jags, where he felt he had to dish out months of good parenting in a single serving.

That evening's advice feast was all for Oliver. No wonder he had a stomachache.

Sitting in a semicircle booth at the Chicken In 'N Out, his father talked incessantly about the importance of building friendships, making pals, chums, buddies.

"Once you find your best friend, everything changes. Life gets off its fat butt and jumps into the pool with a great loud splash!"

He pointed across the table with a half-eaten chicken leg. "Look at your sister and Cherise. Peas in a pod, Ollie. That's what they are."

Rachel just rolled her eyes and started giggling in the secret coded way she had with Cherise. It was true they had a great friendship, and deep down, Oliver *was* jealous. He'd settle for even a hint of what they had, but sadly, he knew even that was shooting too high.

"That's all you need, Ollie," his father said, shoveling

soggy succotash into his mouth. "Another pea for your pod."

Oliver made crop circle patterns in his mashed potatoes, hoping his father would just shut up. He was dealing with the burden of his father's advice the same way he always did: with guilt, shame, and a feeling of total inadequacy.

"I do have friends," Oliver said suddenly. "Tomorrow I'll introduce you."

His father's eyes lit up. "That's fantastic," Arthur said. "This is the best news I ever heard! I was starting to think you'd never have any!" To celebrate, he ordered expensive, fattening desserts for everyone.

Oliver didn't even touch his.

It was late and Oliver still couldn't sleep. The aftertaste of the awful evening was keeping him up, and now he sat outside on the rickety front porch, watching the late-night sky and feeling like a total loser. The only comfort came from Mooch, who lay curled in a question mark on his lap. Oliver stroked the salamander's cool back as he thought about the fictitious friends he couldn't produce.

Oliver sighed. He still had to spend the next day making feeble excuses to his father about his buddies who unexpectedly didn't show up. He'd make up names, or better yet, steal characters from some of his favorite TV shows. Whatever would get him through.

Beep-beep. Beep-beep. Oliver's watch went off on the hour. It was two A.M.

An owl hooted from somewhere in the sky. Oliver noticed that the sounds of the Pond were less orchestrated in the fall. If summer was a full symphony, fall's music was much more like an occasional quartet of strings. Lovely, quiet, and calm.

Mooch had dozed off. He dreamed, as he often did, of the Forbidden Zone, The People Place where, in his sleep, he often walked smiling among the humans.

Oliver finally dropped off, too. His mind drifted aimlessly through snippets of dreams. Nothing lasted, though—a quick warm dream of his grandmother here, an I-forgot-to-wear-pants-to-school dream there. Finally he landed inside a dream that wasn't his at all.

It was as if Oliver and Mooch's brains had connected, and they were somehow watching the same dream unfold. The only difference was, Mooch couldn't see himself. In *his* dream, he could only see the humans who were watching him, and that included Oliver.

Oliver watched Mooch wander through town, happy and smiling. As in most dreams, Oliver had no idea what to make of what he saw. It was a foreign film with no apparent meaning. And then Mooch turned to taste something that smelled yummy, and suddenly there was Oliver holding a simmering steak.

"I'm hungry," Mooch said to Oliver in the dream.

"Mooch, you look awesome!" Oliver responded.

And for the first time in one of his own dreams, Mooch saw what Oliver had been seeing all along. In the reflection of a store's glass window, he was walking upright on two stubby salamander feet.

They woke up simultaneously. "I had the weirdest dream," they said in unison.

It had gotten really cold outside. But neither was feeling it. The rush of excitement they shared was coursing through them like electricity. They didn't speak of it, but both knew what was going to happen. And as the first rays of the day peeked above the distant horizon, they went into the house, determined to make their dream come true.

When Rachel and Cherise finally woke up, it was already 10:30 in the morning. They had stayed up past midnight, swapping stories about the school year, gossiping about kids they knew, giggling about boys.

Now that they were awake, the girl talk continued as if they'd never stopped gabbing.

"So, Rachel, tell me. Anything really wild happen to you since you got here?"

Cherise had just told the story of how she'd made out with Glen Gleason for twenty minutes at a way-boring party.

Rachel bit her lower lip. The only boy she'd been with was Brody Shrank—and she'd been a frog then. But her real secret was too big to keep to herself. "Well, there is one thing. It just happened this week."

Cherise scooted closer. This was going to be good.

Rachel looked her friend in the eyes and smiled. "Okay, you know how I hate slimy bugs and stuff? . . ."

Crash!

The girls jumped to their feet at the sound of something metal being kicked and crunched, followed by the unmistakable voice of a boy screaming, "Bye-bye birdcage!"

Oliver's bedroom door burst open, and Rachel and Cherise were stopped cold. There was Oliver, grinning. His room was a mess. The birdcage lay in a twisted wreck by his desk. Clothes were scattered everywhere. But the strangest sight the girls saw was standing next to Oliver. Two boys: one chubby and wide-eyed, the other lanky and smirking like a maniac. Both in underpants and T-shirts that Rachel immediately recognized as Oliver's.

"Ladies," Oliver said with a casual sweep of his hand. "Meet my two best friends. Mooch and Antoine."

Rachel nearly fainted.

CHAPTER TWENTY-ONE

INKY HAD A DILEMMA. It was his turn to watch the road. But The General had just given him an important secret task. It was practically an order! He chewed on his dusty tail, lost in thought.

The answer came to him slowly. It would be deceitful, but he'd been waiting for The General to give him an assignment, and here it was. Of course he'd do whatever it took.

And so, as Hinky slinked away from the Pond and

across the road toward his covert destination, Pudge marched back and forth at the head of No-way Way. He had gladly taken the skunk's sentry duty turn.

"I'm just happy you realized the truth," said a relieved Pudge. "The General only cares about one thing."

"I know. I know," Hinky had replied, pretending to agree. "The General cares about The General. You really called this one right, Pudge. To think, I came so close to his, his . . . *evil*." Hinky did a great acting job. He almost even brought a tear to his good eye.

"Well, I'd better get going. Can't keep my cousins waiting. Thanks again, Pudge. I owe you one."

Pudge called out as his friend disappeared in the thicket. "You've owed me one since the first time I saved your stinky butt."

The raccoon laughed while Hinky felt the sour lie grow inside his gut.

It was noon by the time the rental car swerved onto the gravel of No-way Way. Pudge calmly yelled out the standard "Code Yellow" warning as he watched the dust settle back on the road. There was no need for panic. It was just a careless human intruder.

"I can't believe what an idiot you are," Rachel said, pulling Oliver aside. They were outside the house waiting for their father, on his way to spend the afternoon with Oliver's new best buds.

"Turning your pets into people?" Rachel continued. "What are you thinking?"

"Don't be so narrow-minded. How about a little enthusiasm on your part?" Oliver replied. "Animal to human; do you know what this means?"

"That you're insane? They're freaks!"

Oliver looked over and watched Mooch test his human tongue by sticking it in and out, while Antoine swayed in the breeze hoping to get the hang of how arms really work.

"They aren't freaks. They're my friends." Oliver retorted. "The other peas in my pod."

"Peas?" Mooch cried out. "I'm starved."

A toot of a car horn put an end to the argument.

"Is that your father?" Cherise said hopefully as a car rounded the last turn of the dirt road. "Please let it be your father." It was obvious how uncomfortable she was around Mooch and Antoine, which Oliver enjoyed immensely.

Arthur stopped the car and hopped out of the driver's side. He was all smiles and his eyes were open just a little too wide—a sure sign to Oliver and Rachel that their father had a bad-news bomb to drop.

"Be back in a jiffy," Arthur said as he walked up the steps and disappeared inside the house.

Oliver looked through the window and watched his parents have one of their fights. He couldn't tell what was being said, but he was sure his father had done something stupid.

Cherise slid inside the car. Anything to get away from the two weirdos. But Antoine decided that the front seat was where the action was and wasted no time making sure he ended up next to her.

"I like what I see," he crowed at the stunned girl, who slid as far away from Antoine as she could.

Rachel reached from the backseat and smacked Antoine on the head. "Keep your claws off my friend. Got it?"

"Watch it, you animal!" he replied, slumping way down into the front seat to avoid being hit again.

"It takes one to know one," Rachel shot back, just before Oliver shoved an elbow into her ribs.

The driver's door opened and Arthur eased inside. "Okay. Slight change of plans," he said glibly. "Sorry to let you down, but a little work emergency popped up. Looks like you guys are on your own for the day."

He didn't notice the relief on his kids' faces. And when he opened his wallet and held out two twenty-dollar bills, it was Antoine who reacted first.

"*Caaawww!* Not a problem. Your dough is safe in my bank." He grabbed the cash and stuffed it into the oversized jeans he was wearing. "Thanks, Mr. D."

As they drove off, Arthur glanced at Oliver in the rearview mirror. "It's great to finally meet your friends, Ollie. Really great."

"You mean *really weird*," added Rachel, right before Antoine turned around and tried to bite her.

The car sprayed loose gravel as it sped jerkily up the dirt road, narrowly missing Pudge, who had to jump to the safety of the ferns. At the end of the road, the car turned right, then drove off toward the center of Little Falls.

"I'll just dump, er, *drop* you kids off in town. You'll have a ball."

Not wanting to risk getting sucked into a conversation with Rachel's dad, Cherise turned on the radio and found a half-decent song. Liking what he heard, Antoine seized the knob and cranked the music up loud. The beat blared against the closed windows. Arthur cringed at the noise and Mooch blocked his ears, but Antoine just started singing along, making up his own words to fit the thumping beat.

"I wanna, wanna, wanna be a big fat green iguana!"

Cherise actually smiled. He was murdering the lyrics, but this nutcase could kind of sing. Rachel felt differently. She wasn't happy having Antoine in the same species, let alone the same car.

But Oliver was happy. He sat in the middle of the backseat, surrounded, almost for the first time ever, by friends.

It was a feeling no one could take away. Not his bossy sister or his distant father. Not even the dark-winged figure above them, closely following the car.

* * *

The last time Hinky had been to the garbage dump was two years ago, when G.R.O.S.S. (the Grand Rank Order of Stinky Skunks) had chosen the site for its annual meeting. Hinky fondly remembered the heat of that August weekend. The festering old garbage had smelled worse than the odor of thirty-five stinky skunks, and just the thought of that sweet, mingling aroma made him swoon.

His task was pretty simple. Or so The General had made it sound. He had to find some specific things to help the plan against the humans. What exactly that plan was, Hinky hadn't a clue. The General only gave him little pieces of the puzzle to gnaw on, so like most things in Hinky's tiny brain, the big picture totally eluded him.

But he was a good soldier and did exactly what he was told. He set out immediately to look for discarded plastic bottles with the strange design on the label. The design he sought out was that of a human skull—the indication that the bottle's contents were poison.

If Reggie, the garbage crew's unofficial boss, had had any idea that the skunk was working for The General, he'd have ordered the other crew crows to attack Hinky with crusty old sneakers and moldy food. But all Reggie saw from the comfort of his perch on top of his mountain of broken filth was another foraging animal, most likely looking for something to eat.

Big mistake.

* * *

Mooch was in heaven. "This is the best steak I ever had."

Oliver laughed, watching his friend gnaw cartoonishly at the slab of meat. "Mooch. That's the *only* steak you've ever had."

They were squeezed into a red vinyl booth in the back of Big Chief's Diner, the greasy spoon located on Main Street between the thimble-sized post office and Ethel's Beauty Hut. To call it a restaurant would be too grand. But it was the best (if not only) place to get a cheap steak, or overcooked eggs, or really crisp, crinkly-cut fries.

The girls had gone to the bathroom together, which Antoine assumed meant they were talking about him. He brushed the hair from his eyes and leaned across the Formica table, smiling with satisfaction. "That Cherise. Wow! Fatboy got his steak and I got me a girlfriend."

Oliver rolled his eyes. Even though he'd never had one, he certainly knew enough about how the process worked to say, "A twenty-minute car ride doesn't make her your girlfriend, dummy."

But Antoine just lifted the sugar dispenser and emptied a swig-full into his mouth. "*Cawww!* She digs me, Ollie. She digs me."

Mooch was guzzling a soda. The sweet flavor combined with the bubbly sensation was new to his amphibian taste buds, and he couldn't stop pouring it down his throat.

"Slow down, Mooch. That stuff is potent."

Oliver's warning came too late. Mooch erupted with a belch that was so loud, Pudge had probably heard it back at the Pond! The aftershock of the beverage took Mooch so by surprise, he thought he'd broken his new boy body.

"That was nice. Real nice." Rachel squeezed back into the booth, actually smiling at the embarrassment on Mooch's round face. To counter his awkward feelings, Rachel did an unexpected thing. She took a quick slug of soda and burped too.

Outside, a lone dark figure was perched on the phone wire, with a perfect bird's-eye view of the diner booth. Though The General had no idea who the rest of the kids were, he recognized Oliver as his intended target. The boy who had been a bird held a key to something the menacing crow craved. Power. And though he had no idea where the kid's strange ability came from, The General silently vowed it would be his.

French fries were followed by apple pie, onion rings, double chocolate cake, and a strawberry milk shake with five straws.

"I think I just gained a dress size," Rachel lamented, grabbing the last fry and dipping it into a pile of ketchup.

Sighing with satisfaction, Oliver wiped off his

milk-shake mustache and went up to pay the bill, while Cherise tossed questions at the two odd boys.

"So what, did you guys, like, grow up here?"

"Um. Yup. Near the Pond." Mooch managed to say, unable to look Cherise in the eye.

"*Him* maybe," Antoine scoffed condescendingly. "I of course was born in a tree."

Rachel kicked him under the table. He was even more of a buffoon as a person than as a crow.

Cherise pushed on. "And you go to school with Oliver?"

Mooch had spaced out on the conversation. His focus had shifted to the ladybug that had landed on the napkin dispenser. Even after all that food, he was still hungry.

"School? Please." Antoine just wouldn't shut up. "I was in the military. Honorable discharge, you know."

Cherise wasn't sure he was kidding or not. "Military? You're, like, what? Twelve?"

But Antoine didn't get a chance to respond, because both girls suddenly watched Mooch pinch a ladybug in his stubby fingers and eat it with an audible *crunch*.

"Mmmm. Tasty."

Rachel exploded. "That's it. We're out of here."

She grabbed Mooch by the hand and pulled him away from the table. Cherise followed them out of the diner, with love-struck Antoine lurking in her shadow.

Unfortunately, downtown Little Falls offered little or

nothing for a kid to do. They weren't getting picked up until 5:30, and it was only 2:15.

"Two-sixteen!" Mooch called out, staring intently at the digital watch he'd begged Rachel to let him wear. She had gladly obliged. Having him fixate on time was far preferable to having him act like a brain case and scarf down anything with six legs.

They decided to go hang out in the town park that was just off the main drag. It was a grass-covered square with a dried-up fountain, a broken swing set, and lots of space to do nothing.

Oliver watched his two pals walk ahead of him and noticed, as surely anyone in town that afternoon would, how oddly they moved. He wondered if he looked as ridiculous to the animals when he was one of them.

Mooch waddled side to side with small steps. Antoine's gait was another story. With hunched shoulders and his neck slightly bent, he extended each leg fully in quick steps. His movement was stilted and peculiar, and somehow came off as cool.

Antoine heard the girls giggling, which inspired him to work up a beat that matched his crow-boy stride. "Cha-caw boom-boom. Cha-cha *cawww* . . . boom-boom . . ."

He started moving to his own rhythm, grooving as though he'd been born for this.

"I wanna, wanna, wanna be a big fat green iguana! Fly above the clouds, you wanna? Singing songs all day. I wanna, wanna, wanna watch the sun set on the water. Hold your hand, I really wanna. Be your friend always."

Rachel gave up. Cherise was now dancing. Oliver was banging on a trash can with a stick he'd picked up. Even Mooch had joined in, clapping out the beats as best he could. They'd started a jam session much to the dismay of the few passersby.

As the raucous clanging and clapping continued, Antoine suddenly climbed onto a park bench, grabbed a low-hanging branch, and swung himself up into the elm tree.

"*Caaaaawwwwww! Caaaawwwww! Caaaawwwww!*"

Cherise pulled Rachel aside. "Okay. Now *that* is weird."

High above the impromptu concert, The General circled slowly in the sky. He wanted to choose his moment carefully. Preferably when the boy was separated from his silly brood. That's when he would strike and find out what secrets the vile human possessed and force him to relinquish the power—or suffer the consequences.

The annoying crowlike "caws" drew his attention immediately.

"What on earth is that awful sound?" The General glided lower, trying to assess his tactical position.

Mooch had pulled Oliver aside. "Thank you," the salamander said, with the hint of a tear starting to form in his saucer eyes. "I've dreamed of this forever. This has been perfect. Totally perfect. An awesome day."

Oliver didn't know what to say. He wasn't good with emotional stuff. "Hey, come on, Mooch. You showed me around your way—this is the least I could do."

Mooch bit his lip. After an uncomfortable pause he finally coughed it out. "Listen, Oliver, would you do me a favor? Would you let me stay like this, you know, like, for always?"

Oliver looked at Mooch. There stood a boy who would probably be as much of an outcast in school as Oliver. As much as Oliver would love to have Mooch as his human best friend, he knew the truth: Mooch would be just as miserable as he was.

The General was gliding now, his wide wings outstretched to ride a strong, southerly wind.

"Aha!" he cried, seeing Oliver and Mooch. "Just the boy and that other fat one. This will be too easy."

Using the wind to propel him, The General turned his body into a black missile—wings tucked tight to his taut belly, his beak ready to strike and slash.

"Mooch, I gotta be honest. Being a kid, a *real* kid—it kinda bites."

"*Cawwwwwwwww!*"

The loud crow call pierced the air as, out of nowhere, a black blur torpedoed through the park. The girls froze. Antoine shut up. And Oliver felt something sharp hit his head before collapsing to the ground in pain.

For Rachel, seeing another bird attack brought

back the memory of that very first day at the house. She trembled in fear and sank behind the park bench, unable to even scream.

The General propelled himself into the air with two strong thrusts before arcing around for a second hit.

Mooch crouched by Oliver's side. Oliver was bleeding from behind his ear. It was a small cut but the pain was enough to make him shout when Mooch touched it.

"*Oww* . . . What happened? What was that?"

Mooch wasn't sure. He'd seen it happen, of course, but was it a bird? A bat?

"I'll tell you what that was," called Antoine, rushing over with Cherise. "That was my uncle!"

Cherise laughed. "Your uncle? Right. And my aunt is a koala bear."

But there was no time for explanations, because the battle cry rocked out again.

"*Ca-Cawwwwwww!*" The General was determined now; he didn't care that the others were near the boy. The boy was wounded and victory was seconds away.

Oliver's hand was coated in blood. The sticky mess frightened him more than the pain, and he felt himself starting to hyperventilate.

Sensing Oliver's panic, Mooch held his buddy's hand.

Antoine grabbed Cherise and hurled her protectively onto the ground. Then he got to his feet, creating a human shield between his uncle and his friends.

"No!" Antoine screamed as his uncle's warriorlike shouts pierced the air.

But The General was crazy with the passion to inflict pain, and relished the sight of this foolish child acting so bravely. And for what? A friend? What a ridiculous reason to die!

Antoine watched as his uncle sped closer and closer. He'd been trained to fight in situations of all kinds and, somewhere deep in his crow brain, he hoped he'd remember the drill that might help him escape injury.

"What to do? What to do? What to do?" Frantic, Antoine flapped his arms like wings as his brain raced over every half-learned thing he'd been taught. But nothing popped into his head. He had no choice but to act on instinct. As The General made his final approach, Antoine grabbed Cherise's purse and swung it around and around as fast as he could.

The General laughed as he saw the pathetic kid twirling the bag. If anything, the sight inspired a final burst of speed, and his aim became even more precise. He'd hit this fool in the chest and then come back for the boy.

But the unexpected impact of the purse's centrifugal force put a quick end to The General's war games. He spun out of control, smashing into the tree next to the bench where Rachel was hiding.

He hit the ground with a dull thud. Rachel could only stare at the bird, afraid she would be the next target of his wrath.

Antoine ran over to Rachel and extended a hand to her. "It's okay. It's all okay."

She smiled weakly. "Thank you."

Antoine helped her up and looked at The General, still lying stunned on the ground. "Leave my friends alone," he said quietly. "Or else."

And as the boy rushed off to join his friends, The General muttered in astonishment, "Antoine?"

The car ride home was less lively than the trip into town. Oliver was still in pain, but the bleeding had stopped. They'd bought some antibacterial ointment at the drugstore and a box of colorful Band-Aids. Mooch and Antoine were both so intrigued by the whole concept of covering wounds with plastic sticky things that each wore half a dozen as medals of their combat.

They silently agreed not to tell Cherise the truth, so they all stuck to the same story: a wild crow attacked Oliver for no apparent reason.

But Antoine had told Oliver and Mooch everything about his uncle. How he hated all humans and orchestrated the attack on Oliver's family. Antoine even confessed that he had been the one who'd bitten Oliver's nose.

"And he made me attack you on the roof, too. I'm so sorry."

"I'm glad about that," Oliver replied. "If you hadn't tried to hurt me, none of us would be friends, right?"

They rode on in silence for a few miles. By the time they turned onto No-way Way, Oliver's father finally spoke.

"You can't imagine the mess I walked into today. A power outage caused the lab's climate system to go totally haywire, which normally would be no big deal. But this place is new. Backup systems not up and running yet."

Oliver let his father's blabbering wash over him. Zoning out helped take his mind off the pain behind his ear.

"Technicians were scrambling everywhere to preserve the specimens. Saved a bunch of 'em, too. But you kids should've seen the ones that didn't make it. It got so cold in one room a frog was frozen solid. And two salamanders died of heatstroke."

Mooch gulped. What kind of a madman was this guy?

"Thankfully, the place is up and running. In fact . . ."

"Cawww!" A black shape hit the windshield and clung to the edge of the car's roof.

It was The General. He was weaker. But he was also angrier than Antoine had ever seen him before.

"Leave us alone," Antoine shouted, banging the windshield with his fist.

But the large crow held fast, peering through the glass. Oliver's dad honked the horn as he attempted to keep the car on the narrow dirt road.

"I see now what I was too dumb to notice," The General shrieked, staring at Antoine. "One of them. My nephew. One of *them!*"

Thud. A dull bump brought the car to a stop. They had gone off the road and into a ditch. Something had hit the tire.

The General flew off, calling, "No one is safe. No one!"

Those who understood the crow felt the terror of his warning. He would be back, and someone would surely pay.

Oliver watched his father jump out of the car to assess the damage. "I know it's a rental, but—" He was looking down at the ground.

The others emptied the car, and then they saw it too. A dead raccoon lying in the dirt.

Although it was a sad sight for them all, Mooch and Antoine were stunned.

Pudge was dead.

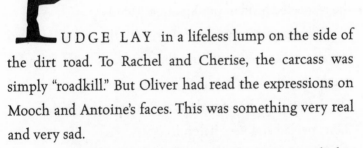

CHAPTER TWENTY-TWO

PUDGE LAY in a lifeless lump on the side of the dirt road. To Rachel and Cherise, the carcass was simply "roadkill." But Oliver had read the expressions on Mooch and Antoine's faces. This was something very real and very sad.

"Guys? You okay?" Oliver tried to approach his friends, but both recoiled from his touch, as if he were somehow to blame.

When the food chain claims another victim, the Pond acknowledges the loss with the understanding that this is just how things must be. Live and let live. Eat or be eaten.

Mooch and Antoine knew the rules. Life comes and goes and sometimes tastes real good.

But death caused by a human was always upsetting, and it was exactly this kind of barbaric behavior that incensed The General and fueled the Elders way of thinking. "Humans are careless, thoughtless killers."

In life, Pudge was just another small animal. But in death, he was about to become bigger than he could have ever imagined.

Word of the killing spread around the Pond with a staccato beat *tap-tap-tap*ped from the tallest branch of the oldest tree. The woods were alive with renewed anger and fear of the humans and their murderous ways. Emotions were running high. This wasn't just another casualty—Pudge was the respected head of the Mammal Family.

Perhaps the only one pleased with the announcement was the dark crow watching the emotions build from his perch atop the nearby cliffs. "This is an unexpected boost," The General said to Shadow, the crow cadet by his side. "Unexpected and very helpful."

Mooch and Antoine had wasted no time shedding their boy bodies. Now they stood by the steel-gray water, staring silently at the darkening sky.

"We all gotta go sometime," Mooch said. "But Pudge . . ."

"Yeah, I know. This just wasn't his time." Antoine was slowly stirring the shallow water with his claw. "And we were one of *them* when it happened. It kind of makes me sick."

Mooch had to agree. Suddenly he felt guilty for ever having wanted to be a human.

It was almost sundown, time to gather for the Remembrance Ritual, a ceremony held when any Alliance leader died.

"Catch you there, Mooch." Antoine raised his head and flew off, calling to a group of crows in the dusk-cloaked horizon.

Oliver finally spoke up. He'd been hanging back from his friends, feeling the awkward distance between them.

"I'm coming with you," Oliver said, gripping the gem in his hand.

"No. Not this time." Mooch didn't even turn around to look up at the boy towering above him. "You wouldn't understand this. You don't belong."

Oliver stood silent as Mooch slithered off. Abandoned, he became instantly aware of how cold it had become. He shoved his hands deep into his sweatshirt pockets and watched white clouds of his breath expand into the autumn night.

"Stupid thing." Oliver pulled back his arm, ready to toss the gem into the middle of the pond. He felt betrayed by the magic. It had unlocked a world filled with new friends and hope, and now he felt shut out, back in the lonely place he knew too well.

Pudge was in the same spot where he had landed after being hit by the car. It wasn't a pretty sight, but moving the body was strictly against the custom.

"The worst part is," croaked Frankie, the Amphibian Elder, who formed part of the inner circle surrounding the body. "Pudge woulda hated this."

Fat Mama spoke up. "No one wants to die. It's just part of the cycle."

The bloated frog turned to the spider. "I ain't talking about hating the dying part. I'm talking about the food."

"What food?"

"Exactly my point." Frankie smiled. "There ain't any. Pudge woulda been pissed."

And that was how it was supposed to go. The Remembrance Ritual was all about memories: sad, happy, funny, dumb. It didn't matter what was said as long as it had some connection to the one who had died.

Beyond the inner circle of Pond Elders, creatures were gathered in clusters of species. Bugs hung with bugs. Birds perched with birds. And though he hadn't done it for a long time, Mooch now stood with the other salamanders.

"He sure was a loud snorer."

"One time I saw him fall out of a tree cuz he fell asleep up there."

"Pudge once stole every scrap of food I'd saved for the winter. What a character."

"Hey, Mooch." A recognizable voice whispered near the salamander. "Remember how he was the one who got us together?"

Mooch turned slowly from his kin and looked into the dark weeds behind him. He didn't see anything, but knew right away whose voice had spoken. "Willy? You in there?"

A moment later the dragonfly flew out from the thicket. The hum of his wings reminded Mooch of their past.

"Hey."

"Hey."

The unspoken anger and hurt between them drifted aside. They were both there remembering Pudge, which was like remembering their own friendship; a friendship that never would've even existed without the raccoon. Pudge was the one who had stood up to the Alliance and insisted that the Pond change its old rules and let children mix and mingle and play outside of their own species. That's how Willy and Mooch had first met, when the Alliance reluctantly okayed Pudge's request.

"How's it going?" Mooch asked. "Haven't seen you much lately."

"Yeah, well, I've been pretty busy," Willy lied. "How about you? You doing okay?"

Mooch shrugged. "Not bad. I guess. But Pudge . . ."

"I know, man. I know."

And just like that, the salamander and dragonfly felt their worlds reconnect.

"Brrrr," Oliver shivered, blowing warm air into his cupped hands.

He was cold and bored, waiting by the rock. He wished whatever it was he wasn't allowed to be part of would just hurry up and be finished. His nose was running and he had to keep wiggling his toes to keep his feet warm. He didn't want to go inside the house, though. Didn't want to get sucked into the vortex of whatever his parents were talking about.

To get his blood circulating he wrapped his sweatshirt tightly around himself and decided to walk along the outer Pond. He'd often explored this same path as a salamander, and was surprised to realize how different it felt doing the hike as a boy.

Instead of the minute details of the ground, he was seeing the entire expanse of the pond, the wide sky and far-stretching woods. A thought spread inside, and Oliver realized that he was looking at his own life from a new perspective too, seeing himself from the point of view of someone looking at the whole, not the tiny awful details that on their own had always made him feel bad.

For the first time ever, Oliver saw that he could make this choice. He could decide either to see himself as a sad boy locked in his bedroom watching TV, hiding from the world—or he could see himself as someone outside, exploring the world, watching the stars, imagining great things.

He sucked in the chilly night air through smiling teeth, amazed at how warm he felt.

The voices stopped him cold.

"Yes, my friend. This is our night."

His first impulse was to turn back, but Oliver knew that voice. He just couldn't put a face to it. Carefully, he crouched behind the remaining brown cattail reeds, hoping to overhear more.

"You got what I asked for? You placed it where I told you?"

The other voice said, "Yes, they must pay for this. Human blood must spill!"

This other creature was upset now, practically shouting. "Why was it Pudge? I was helping you—he was helping me. It should've been *me*."

Oliver realized they were talking about the raccoon. But who were these two? And what plot were they discussing?

Oliver parted the reeds just an inch or so. The slice of moon cast a vague glow, and he had to concentrate hard to see. The shapes of two creatures began to take form: one low to the ground, one upright and unmistakably birdlike.

"First the Alliance falls, and then the humans will pay. Stick with me, Hinky. Power shall be our destiny!"

"But what if they won't listen? What if they won't make the spider step down?"

The voice, the one Oliver knew, laughed. "Then, my friend, we kill whoever gets in our way."

And then the wings opened and, even in shadow, Oliver realized who it was. The crow! Oliver felt his ear throb in recognition.

The other creature had begun to cry, and Oliver gasped as the crow's wing swooped down and struck its head.

"Get a grip, you fool. Your emotions have no place now. Actions are what we need to erase the past and move gloriously into our future! Let's go!"

The crow flew off, and the other creature let loose one last sob before hurrying toward what Oliver could only imagine would be a horrible bloodbath of some kind. He had to do something. He sensed his old self tugging at his sleeve, whispering that he should just go home and hide in his room. But his new self felt strong and needed. He jammed his hand inside his pocket and retrieved the gem. He knew he didn't have much time, so he looked quickly for any creature to transform with.

The ribbon snake never knew what hit him.

CHAPTER TWENTY-THREE

H INKY TOOK a deep breath before pushing his way into the center of the circle. All he wanted to do was keep it together, but his tears fell hotly onto the dull coat of the raccoon, who was dead because Hinky had lied and gone to help The General in his own illicit scheme.

The only thing that provided any relief was knowing that Pudge had been killed by a human.

Farther off in the woods, Oliver realized his mistake almost instantly. By transforming into a snake, he had chosen a tedious form of travel. Certainly in a calmer moment he'd have tried to become a fast-footed squirrel or perhaps even a sleek, winged bug. But he'd acted too quickly, and as a consequence, now could only slither toward the dirt road and the raccoon. He needed to find Antoine or Mooch. He hoped they'd know what to do.

After what felt like hours of belly-scraping travel, Oliver found himself poking through the circle of creatures that ringed the dirt road. He wasn't sure what he would do, he just knew that he had to protect his friends.

The General stood slightly apart from the others with the self-satisfied knowledge that he'd put every cog and gear in place, and he just had to wait. And then—all would be his.

The General saw the slender yellow-striped snake who'd inched into the ceremony. The crow had no reason to suspect that he was looking at the boy. Instead he just smiled, imagining how good that slinky snack would taste. Later.

Oliver slithered through the crowd. Oddly, for the first time since using the gem, he felt incredibly out of place. It was as if the snake skin he was stuffed inside didn't fit right. Maybe Mooch had been right. He didn't belong here. Maybe he'd overreacted to what he'd heard by the Pond. Maybe he had simply stumbled onto a playful game between friends.

But then he saw the crow, The General, who was

smiling to himself with an almost gluttonous grin that sent a shiver through every coil of Oliver's elongated body.

No, thought Oliver. I know what I heard and I have to stop him.

Oliver quickly scanned the group for Mooch. His neck ached as he pushed and peered into so many unknown faces. And then, there he was—Mooch—standing next to a hovering dragonfly.

"Mooch, finally. Listen to me."

"Oliver?" The salamander whipped around, and was caught off guard to be eye-to-eye with a snake. "What are you doing here? I asked you not to come."

At first, Oliver was unsure how to react. But he took a deep breath and pushed on.

"Look. I know what you said. But, Mooch, you've got to listen to me. Something awful is going on. . . ."

But Mooch couldn't listen. Thinking about Pudge had stirred old memories inside him. His feelings were raw and his sadness was something he didn't want to share. He turned his back on Oliver and walked away.

"Take it from me. Just give him some space." Willy landed next to the snake. And even though the dragonfly still resented Oliver, he tried to be positive.

"It's been a pretty emotional night. He'll come around."

Oliver spoke urgently. "Well, it's gonna get a whole lot more emotional around here. The big crow—he's got some kind of plan. He said—"

But Oliver wasn't able to explain anything else. The gathering was interrupted by a huge wailing cry from the woods.

"More fish! Dead! More fish!"

Hearing this news brought even more creatures out from their homes. The crowd swelled with those both curious and angry. First Pudge, now this. What else would arise to disturb the relative peace of their Pond?

The only one who knew that answer was The General, who slowly cleaned his left talon, biding his time. Waiting for his moment.

Two young crow cadets swooped into the circle. "It's awful! Just awful!" They appeared distraught, giving The General the secret satisfaction of seeing how much their acting lessons had paid off.

Fat Mama dropped to the ground and assumed her authority, trying to calm the crowd.

"Attention. Everyone. Let's take a moment to assess the facts." She then turned to the crows. "Now, please, tell us all what you saw."

The cadet named Shadow spoke first. He looked slowly from Elder to Elder. He made sure to remember to let his voice shake and tremble as he spoke.

"It's happening again. Fish are being killed by the humans. Poisons. We found the proof!"

"Proof?" Fat Mama was still in control of the crowd, but just barely. She eyed the crow with suspicion. "What proof?"

And then it was Hinky's turn. He wiped his tears with his paw and darted into the wooded thicket. He was gone for a full minute.

All eyes were on Hinky as he reemerged onto the road. A gasp of fear rose from the creatures when they saw what he pushed into the circle. It was a large plastic container. A bottle immediately recognized by all as poisonous.

"I found this last week, floating near the mudflats," he lied. "I didn't want to scare anyone so I kept quiet. But now the truth must be told. The people are trying to kill us."

And then he cried. He cried for the Pond. He cried for his lies. He cried for Pudge, who would never again be able to tell him that what he was now doing was so terribly wrong.

"The people? The ones in the house?" croaked Frankie, which got the Amphibians to start making some noise.

At Flake's signal the Reptiles joined in, banging on all the turtles' shells in a rousing rhythm of support, (which conveniently alleviated the raw itch on the Elder Leader's backside).

"There's more containers, too," added Shadow. "Lots and lots."

As if on cue, half a dozen crow cadets emerged, pushing and tugging evidence to support the theory: that the humans were polluting the Pond.

Oliver turned to Willy, who had a worried look on his face. "This is such a lie. There is no poison in the water."

Then the bawling started. Young beetles and toads clung to their mothers, afraid and worried for their future. Birds and squirrels broke into sobs. And Fat Mama, standing in the center of it all, watched her control of the Alliance begin to unravel.

The General was ecstatic.

CHAPTER TWENTY-FOUR

AFTER WALKING away from Oliver, Mooch had wandered aimlessly into the woods and curled up inside a rotting birch log. The mushy pulp smelled good and reminded him of the old hiding place he and Willy had made under the maple tree.

It all seemed so long ago. He thought about the strange events of the last few months that had led to this moment. Being kidnapping by the kid bugs. Oliver grabbing him by the Pond. The golden magic of the gem that had finally allowed him to experience the world in human form.

He sighed. It was all so fantastic, a wonderful adventure. But what did it all mean? And why did he feel so unsettled?

As he dug a small hole in the fresh, soft wood, a deep longing overwhelmed him. Running into Willy had brought back the memory of his former life. How different he now felt from before—before he'd been captured by Oliver. Living in the house and getting to know Oliver had made a huge difference in his life, and it was an experience he'd never trade—not for all the gooey worms in the world. But that nagging feeling inside . . .

Mooch knew what the feeling was. It was hard to accept, but he knew he would not be going back to live in the house. His world was outside. His home was the Pond.

As if to reward this revelation, a fly landed just to the right of his round shoulder, and in one quick instinctive move, Mooch swallowed the tasty treat whole.

"Please. Stop. Everyone, just stop!" Fat Mama was trembling. The creatures of the Pond had always looked to her for answers, but now they seemed to be looking for blame.

"What are we going to do? Just let them slaughter us with their poison again?"

"Humans are evil."

"My babies will not be killed without a fight from me!"

Oliver watched it all numbly. Chaos was erupting

around him, and though he didn't have an understanding of the workings of the Alliance, he did know this hysteria was somehow part of whatever plan that crow had in his twisted mind.

"Just a few more minutes," The General whispered to Hinky. "Remember, when I give the signal, then you know what to say."

Hinky nodded. Yes, he knew what to say. He knew what to do.

Willy tapped Oliver on what would've been his shoulder if he hadn't been a snake. "I've got to get you out of here."

Oliver was shocked. "What? No way. I have to stay and help!"

"Please," began the dragonfly. "There's nothing we can do."

But before Willy could stop him Oliver opened his mouth in an attempt to put a stop to the growing pandemonium.

"Wait! It's the crows! They're lying!" He shouted out as loud as he could. "Stop them now!"

Willy cringed as the air became silent and still. "I wish you hadn't done that," he said as he nervously checked the escape routes that he and Oliver might take.

Sensing all eyes on him, Oliver gulped. "Sorry," he whispered to Willy. "Open mouth, insert foot—I mean, tail."

Out of nowhere, The General appeared, dropping with

a whoosh of open wings in front of the snake.

"How dare you insinuate that we are to blame for this *human* mess." The General pinned Oliver to the spot with his gaze.

"Who do you think you are, you pathetic little snake?"

Willy whispered, "Don't say a word."

Oliver wanted to be silent. He clamped his jaws tightly, but a voice rose up from his belly and defiantly burst from his mouth.

"Who am I?" he hissed back, staring up at the dark, towering presence. "I'm the one who knows you are a liar."

A startled hush engulfed the Pond creatures. In the silence, Oliver noticed how The General's beak glistened like a razor blade in the dim moonlight. He dared not even blink as he realized he was just a few quick jabs away from becoming a snake-kabob.

But The General didn't attack. He narrowed his eyes into slits and glared at the snake. And then he did something that took everyone by surprise. He laughed.

"*Caw! Ccaaawww! Cacawwwww!*" The General's roaring cackle was soon echoed by his squadron.

"Silly snake," The General began, working hard not to let his anger show. He then addressed the group. "My friends, this shocking discovery of how the humans want to destroy our Pond has made our friend here upset. Poor little guy."

The General nodded to his cadets, signaling them

to relax their watchful stance. He knew the snake was trouble. But his present war was with the Alliance, so conquering the impertinent reptile would have to wait. The General whirled around and refocused on his master plan.

"Now, let's get back to matters of life and death, shall we?" he said. He had to recharge the fear in them. "Human poison—once again at the Pond. How could things get so bad?"

That was Hinky's cue—but the skunk was lost in the tangle of hateful thoughts. The General tried again.

"I said, how could things get so bad? Hinky? H*inky!*"

"Oh. Yes. If you asked me," Hinky's well-practiced speech began, "it all comes down to um, leadership. Our Alliance is supposed to protect us. Right? It's supposed to make us all feel safe. But the thing is, I don't feel safe. Do you?"

At Willy's nudge, Oliver slithered to the dark edges of the circle. "What's going on here? Why don't they do something?"

"Fear," said Willy. "Fear blocks out thinking. Thinking calmly, anyway."

Fat Mama had regained her composure. "Pond creatures, I appeal to you all. . . ."

But her cry for patience was swallowed into the murmur of dissent.

"No more spider rule!" shouted a voice from the trees. Oliver could tell it was the voice of a crow.

"No more Alliance!" echoed another unseen voice.

Willy was frantic to get Oliver away. "Please. We must leave here. Before it is too late." The small dragonfly practically tugged on the snake's tail. But he was powerless to move Oliver, whose attention was glued to the near-riot before him.

Hinky shouted to all who would listen. "We need new leaders—powerful, strong leaders who will use fighting, not words, to solve our problems!"

"Crows!" a voice boomed out in suggestion.

"Crows!" echoed a chorus of support, some more certain than others.

"No," Fat Mama whispered, already feeling a crushing sense of dread.

Frankie spoke up. "General, it is sudden, we realize. But desperate times and all . . ."

Let them wait, The General told himself. *Let them worry that you will say no.*

Looking across the sea of faces, he saw admiration and hope. Little did they know how much he detested them all.

A cold rain began to fall as the General stepped onto the flat rock to the cheers of the Pond. His moment had arrived and he basked in its hot glow. The roar of approval finally dissipated, giving The General the quiet space to make his acceptance speech. Oh, how he loved the taste of power.

But before he could accept his new position, Oliver rose up next to the rock.

"He is not the one! He is not your friend!"

This time there was no shocked reaction from the crowd. All eyes were on him in hatred. They had made a decision and no one welcomed this sort of interruption.

"I put up with your disrespect before," The General began ominously, "but now you have pushed me to my limits."

What a perfect way to exercise his power; by making an example of someone who dared disagree with his authority.

With a swiftness that caught Oliver off guard, the General grabbed the snake in his claws and held him up for all to see. "Speaking up against me will be your last mistake, you fool."

Oliver had never felt such deep terror before, and he wished he could just transform back into himself and run away fast. But he was too frightened.

"This is what happens when you disobey General Eduardo Ignacio Santo Domingo!" Oliver felt himself being lifted into the air.

Oliver was starting to lose consciousness now. The claws were like steel clamps cutting off his breath. Willy was helpless—all he could do was watch and wait.

The snake's eyes met The General's. "I'm not . . ." Oliver squeezed the words from his throat.

"You're not *what*?" snapped the crow.

The General held Oliver out so that his tail twitched above the heads of the crowd.

His mouth was dry and his breathing was difficult. But Oliver pushed harder than he ever had before to get the last words out.

"I'm . . . not . . . a snake," he whispered. "I'm a . . ." Blackness swirled inside his head and a numbing sensation spread up from the furthest coil of his body. "I'm a . . . *human*," he moaned finally, loud enough to reach the tiniest of shocked ears.

And then he passed out. Oliver's long body became a limp rope in the claws of the startled General, who now only wanted one thing from the snake—the secret of his magical power of transformation.

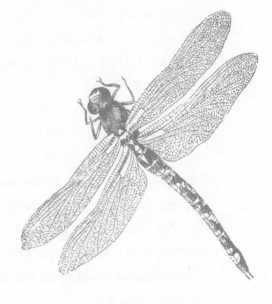

CHAPTER TWENTY-FIVE

"**C**AWWWWW*!*" The General's scream exploded inside Oliver's ears, sending a shiver of fear through his coiled body.

Clinging to the snake, The General flew toward the pointed cliffs that were set back behind the western edge of the Pond. The stone protrusion was called the Crag, and it was a dangerous wall of rock, known for its cramped hiding places and twisted dark caves. It was a location notorious for unexplainable accidents, which was why it was off-limits to most Pond creatures. Not coincidentally, it was also the well-known roost of the Black Angels.

The General flew in through a crevice that was barely large enough to accommodate him. The claustrophobic chasm was perfect for torturing any creature dumb enough to anger him.

Once inside, The General threw the snake against the wall. Coiled in pain, Oliver could see only the red-hot eyes that bore into him.

"Now, let's have us a little chat," The General said in a voice just barely above a whisper. He dragged a claw against the stone floor, sparks shooting out from his talons.

Oliver was terrified but knew he had to strike back before it was too late. In one swift move he sprang forward, his fanged jaws open wide. But he had transformed himself into a nonvenomous ribbon snake. Instead of inflicting pain, he received it, with a hard smack of the crow's wing, which swatted him back to the ground as if he were just a pesky fly.

"I hated you before I even knew why," The General said. "But now that you have something I want, the taste of your blood will be so much sweeter."

Antoine coasted back toward the Remembrance Ritual, after a reflective solo flight around the Pond. His mood was shattered as soon as he saw the chaos.

Crow cadets were everywhere and they were pushing the different species into clumps of frightened hostages.

"Insects, over there. Reptiles, shut up and move it! This is for your own good!"

The Amphibians were being corralled by several mean-tempered crows, who took pleasure pecking and clawing at the scared group.

"You're messing with the wrong frog," belched Frankie, who shut his eyes before snapping his tongue out wildly. It was a direct hit—striking the nearest crow in the eye.

"Ow! Watch it," the crow screamed as he peeled the sticky appendage off his eyeball.

"Yeah, I still got it," the big frog said. "They don't call me 'The Tongue' for nothin'."

The Reptiles were trapped beside a boulder. The Insects cornered in the ditch. Even the other Birds were cowering, frightened and made flightless by their crow brethren.

Antoine landed in the middle of the road, still trying to figure out what had happened.

"What? I can't leave you guys alone for ten minutes before all heck breaks loose?" Antoine joked. But instead of laughter, the response he got was the sharp sting of a rock on his back.

He turned to face the glare of Shadow, the crow cadet who had always hated him when they were training together.

"Whatsa matter?" Shadow said. "Baby's uncle not here to stick up for him?"

Antoine took a bold (and perhaps stupid) step toward the other crow. In the past he would've skulked away, intimidated, but now he felt much more sure of himself.

"Okay, one: look at me." Wing on hip, he struck a muscleman pose he'd seen on a TV infomercial. "I may not have six-pack abs, but I am obviously *not* a baby. And two: my uncle never stood up for me in his life."

"You're a disgrace to the species," Shadow said with a punch to Antoine's gut. He placed a claw on Antoine's neck, pinning him to the ground.

"I hope your uncle will deal with you after he finishes off that human snake."

Antoine sputtered and sat up.

"*Human* snake? What nonsense are you talking about, Shadow?"

Shadow kicked some dirt and rocks in Antoine's direction. "All I know is, some puny snake made The General madder than you ever could. Weirdo claimed he was a human. The General just grabbed the jerk and tore outta here."

Antoine tried to get up, but Shadow shoved him back down with a laugh. "Where do you think you're going, loser? I got specific orders from the top to keep your feathered butt right here."

Antoine's mind raced. Why had Oliver been a snake? Why had he come to the ceremony? And how was he going to overpower Shadow and help his friend?

Across the road, Willy was hunched low to the ground. "I know you have no reason to believe me, but what choice do we have now?" He was whispering to a small circle of insect kids. These were some of the same bugs who'd deserted Willy, who'd gotten tired of being ordered to fight his nonexistent battles.

But they were scared, and for once, Willy's tone was different. He wasn't ordering. He was *asking*. And they all silently agreed—working together was their only hope against the takeover of the crows.

"Ahhhh!"

The pain was so severe, Oliver's mind exploded in a flash of bright silver light.

"I'm sorry. Did that hurt?" The General asked.

The wind had picked up and cold sheets of rain were falling. Oliver's eyes had finally adjusted to the blackness of the space, allowing him to see past The General to the narrow opening in the rocks: his door to freedom.

"What do you want? Why are you doing this to me?" Oliver was close to tears as he backed away from his captor. He felt the crunch of small bones rub against his scales and realized he was not the first creature to fall prey to The General here.

"I want to know the secret. I want to own the power that you have, and I want it NOW!"

In desperation, Oliver slithered away. He pushed his long tail back against the rock wall behind him. Aiming between The General's tall legs, he leaped out fast, like an arrow shooting for a bull's-eye.

"Oww!"

Oliver had almost made it past The General—or at least half of him had. But The General had stopped Oliver's escape, driving his beak like a stake through his tail. Oliver realized he had no choice but to give up.

Once more, The General tossed him against the far wall of the rocky cavern. The crow knew he'd won. The boy was his. It was all just a matter of time.

Antoine was knocked to the rain-soaked ground again. He was no match for Shadow. Continuing this fight would just end up making things worse than they were now—if that were even possible.

"*Psst.* Tough guy. Yeah, you." A tiny, deep voice whispered from somewhere behind Antoine. "Don't move. We got your back."

Antoine tried to crane his neck left, but a sharp pain on his shoulder stopped him.

"Hey, stupid, what part of 'Don't move' don't you understand?"

And though Antoine had no idea what was happening, he was glad to know that someone or some*thing* was on his side.

Mooch felt so much better. He was anxious to apologize to Oliver, to try and explain everything he'd been thinking. Even though earlier in the day he'd begged Oliver to help him stay a human boy forever, now all he wanted was to remain who he was meant to be.

Mooch took a deep breath and crawled across the drenched road toward the house. Oliver will be coming back from the ritual soon, he thought. Mooch already missed the tasty treats Oliver used to steal for him from the kitchen. But there was no turning back. Not even for leftovers.

As he stared up at the house, the front door opened and Oliver's father stepped out into the wet night. Mooch should have dashed into the bushes, but some feeling inside told him to stay.

"Well, look at you," Arthur said, unaware he was staring at the same salamander he'd once met as Oliver's pet. "You're not afraid of me, are you?"

Mooch realized he wasn't afraid, just curious as to why he knew deep in his gut that he was about to let the man stoop down and carry him away.

It was one moment that would change many lives forever.

Mooch gazed out the front window of the car, which slowly bounced and rocked up No-way Way. He wasn't sure what the consequences of this choice would be, he just had a feeling that letting Oliver's father take him was the right thing to do.

The car rounded a twist in the road, and suddenly the headlights shone on the turmoil ahead. Mooch was shocked at the sight of so many crows crowding around the other members of the Pond. Pushing. Yelling. Fighting.

"Would you look at all those birds," Arthur said, gripping the wheel tighter. "Must be the weather."

But Mooch could tell that the weather had nothing to do with this. It was clear that the crows had somehow taken charge of the others. But *why*?

Frozen for a moment in the glare of the headlights, the crows herded their prisoners to the side of the road, and as Mooch looked through the side window, he saw Hinky staring at the car as it passed.

"Murderer! Murderer!" the skunk shouted, which incited the crows to attack the vehicle with their beaks and claws.

As a final act of revenge, Hinky lifted his tail and let loose his disgusting odor, filling the car with the stench. Mooch coughed and rolled his eyes as Arthur turned on the air conditioning, which only sucked the smell in more.

"Willy?"

Mooch stared out the back window, relieved to see his friend. He watched as the dragonfly chased after the car, but Arthur had started driving faster now.

"Mooch! Come back. Mooch!" Willy yelled.

And the last image Mooch saw before the car rounded the corner was the brilliant shimmer of Willy's wings as he raced off to get the only help the dragonfly could think of.

CHAPTER TWENTY-SIX

WILLY NEEDED THE GIRL. He knew the events that were already unfolding would be catastrophic unless he got her help. He also knew that telling her about Oliver would only get in the way. For now, it was best to just convince her—and go.

He'd discovered a way into the house through a cracked window in the living room and was now zipping through the downstairs looking for the sister.

Inside the kitchen, he saw the mother washing dishes at the sink, humming. If she knew the danger her family was in, he thought, she'd be singing a different tune.

"Mo-om," called a girl's voice. "Can you bring us up some sodas?"

Willy didn't wait for the answer. He had to follow that voice.

"Pleeeaaassse?" came the voice again, clearly from upstairs.

Cherise was listening to some new MP3's on Rachel's bedroom computer. She didn't even notice the buzzing wings that briefly darted into the room and then back out.

Rachel stood in the bathroom, staring into the mirror at her hair, which she'd just dyed in thick red stripes. As she turned her head from side to side, trying to decide if the streaks were cool or scary, she noticed a dragonfly zigzagging behind her. Despite her recent experiences with the gem, she was still startled to hear the insect speak.

"Um, listen, I know we haven't exactly met," the dragonfly called to her in the mirror. "But I kind of need your help. We don't have much time."

Rachel rolled her eyes. "Whatever your problem is," she said, "I couldn't care less."

Determined, Willy flew around to face her and fluttered about two inches from her nose. "That man with the car, he took Mooch."

Rachel figured the man was her father and that, most likely, if he took Mooch, it couldn't be good. She remembered that her father had blabbed on about some lab meltdown and realized that he probably planned to use Mooch as some sort of specimen. She didn't want to get involved in another one of Oliver's magic messes. But she couldn't shake off the image of Mooch—that shy, chubby boy eating French fries in the diner. He looked just like any other kid, and Rachel knew that whether he was a boy or a salamander—she couldn't let something awful happen to him.

"A little privacy here, okay?" she said, pulling her bathrobe tighter. "As a species, humans kinda like their bathroom time to themselves."

Willy turned around as Rachel brushed out her hair. "I hate to be dramatic," he continued urgently, "but it's a matter of life and death."

"So is looking good, pal," she said, stalling for time while trying to figure out a plan to sneak out of the house and help rescue the salamander. She stared into the mirror for a minute, then opened the medicine cabinet and took out a small wooden matchbox. Sliding it open she lifted out the fragment of Oliver's crystal—the one she'd gone back for—and slid it into her pocket. If the chipped-off piece contained any magic at all, maybe it would help them tonight.

"Remember, buddy, you're only gonna have one shot, so take your best one. Got me?"

Antoine listened carefully, but was afraid to so much as nod. The mysterious voice from earlier had revealed himself to be the same tough-guy red ant kid who'd ridden atop Mooch when he was captured by the insect kids.

Antoine watched as a half dozen kid spiders crept out of the wet darkness. Silently, they surrounded Shadow, who was distracted by several young hornets dancing around his head.

"Steady. Careful . . ." the red ant whispered from his lookout on the slope of Antoine's black chest.

All Antoine could think about was Oliver in the clutches of the monster that was his uncle. He was alert and ready to do whatever it took to put a stop to The General's plans.

The red ant was ready, too. He gave the signal—which just so happened to be a fierce bite into Antoine's chest. "Owww!" shrieked the startled crow, which was exactly the intended effect.

That's all it took. Shadow turned, and in a split second, the tiny spiders shot their sticky silken strings at him.

The red ant turned to Antoine and shouted, "What are you waiting for? An invitation? Go! Get outta here!" To give him a jump-start, he bit the crow again.

Antoine sprang to his feet and spread his wings against the cold rain, which now seemed to be coating the earth in a thin sheet of ice. He looked around and saw that the crows had successfully divided the Families into five frightened groups. The Fish, safely underwater, were off the hook.

Antoine wanted to help—but that would have to wait. He had to find Oliver. Had to try and save his friend from his uncle.

The car radio was playing Mozart, a soothing sound that mixed oddly with the *clickety-whoosh* of the windshield wipers. Arthur hummed softly with the music, while Mooch listened, perched against the back window. Nestled against a stereo speaker, Mooch closed his eyes and felt the music rumble inside him.

During his eight weeks inside the house, the salamander had assumed that all music was the loud, thumping, ear-splitting noise that Oliver and Rachel played. He had no idea that there was anything outside of nature that sounded as peaceful and beautiful as what was flowing around him in the car.

"What do you say, salamander—are you up for an adventure?" Arthur was looking in his rearview mirror at Mooch, who met his stare and smiled as the music orchestrated their trip into the unknown.

Back atop the Crag, inside the crevice, a slow runoff was trickling into the dark gully where Oliver lay shivering, hurt, and wet.

"Tell me what this power is! I need to know!" The General demanded.

"It's . . . it's . . . a stone. A gem of some kind." Oliver told

The General everything. He had no fight left in him. He just wanted it all to end, to go back to the way it was, before he'd overheard the crow—before he'd found the gem—before he'd left his little bedroom in the city.

"Show me! I want to see this magic thing. Now!"

"It's not that easy," Oliver replied, dizzy with the pain that throbbed in red-hot spasms through his tail. "I have to become me again—a kid. Then I'll have it. I mean, you'll have it. The gem, I mean."

The General took one menacing step closer. "Less talk. More action," he said through a clenched beak.

Oliver tried to control his breathing. He closed his eyes tight, trying with every fiber to shut out where he ached, to ignore the chilling water, to free his mind and become calm so that the magic could swirl inside him and carry him swiftly back into the body that . . .

Oliver's eyes shot open. He couldn't transform. Not inside this cramped space.

"What's taking so long?" The General shrieked, hovering over Oliver with the pointed spear of his beak.

Oliver was panicked. "I—I can't do it."

"Can't or won't?" the crow snapped.

"I literally can't," Oliver said. "Look at this space. It's so small. As a snake, I fit. But when I become me again—my human body will be crushed. There isn't room for a person in here."

The only sound Oliver heard then was the echo of a

vicious wind and the pulse of his own frantic heart.

"Hmmm," replied The General. "You certainly are the lucky one, aren't you?"

Oliver didn't know what the crow meant. He was only certain it wasn't good.

"Yes," he continued. "Lucky, lucky you. You get to choose which way you'd rather die. Shredded snake? Or crushed boy?"

"But if you kill me as a snake," he began, "I don't know what will happen to the gem. Maybe it will just disappear. Then what? Huh?"

Oliver watched The General's face for any sign of doubt. But if Oliver's question troubled him, the crow betrayed nothing. He just grinned wickedly.

"That's just one chance I'm willing to take," The General snarled. His left talon was just a swipe from Oliver's face.

And then Oliver froze with the realization that, with or without the gem, his life was almost over.

CHAPTER TWENTY-SEVEN

RACHEL HAD DRIVEN only one car in her whole fifteen-year-old life. It was the most beautiful thing she'd ever seen. It was robin's-egg blue and had seats that made you feel as though you were sitting on a cloud. It was a ride at Disney World, when she was seven.

"Do you have any clue how much trouble I'm gonna get in for this?" she said, dangling a Marvin the Martian keychain in front of the dragonfly sitting on the dashboard of her mother's car.

"Hey, I'm sorry," Willy said. "But you'll thank me later. Trust me."

Rachel slid the gear into drive and eased the car up the slippery road. "Grounded for life," she muttered, knowing, however, that her mother wouldn't see her stealing the car. Cherise was taking care of that.

"I know I should tell you everything, but there's, like, no way I can," Rachel had told her friend as she quickly threw on some jeans and a sweatshirt.

Cherise just smiled, thinking Rachel's secret mission had to be about a boy. "Apology not needed. Just have fun. What do you need me to do?"

And that's why Rachel knew she had plenty of time to slip away; because Cherise had created a brilliant Mom diversion.

"Ms. T., you are gonna be the hottest teacher in that school," Cherise said, working an entire bottle of "Autumn Fire" hair color into Carol's damp hair.

"Well, I have to admit, I could use a little change," Carol replied giddily, unaware of the dramatic changes *really* happening around her.

"I'll give it to you—I promise," Oliver pleaded with The General. "Just let me outside, where I won't be crushed when I transform. Come on! I'm just a kid!"

"And I'm just a crow who couldn't care less!" The General was truly enjoying the fear that was oozing from

244

his prisoner. "Now, decide! Which way would you like to die?"

Oliver could no longer feel the tip of his tail. Whether it was because of his throbbing wound or the puddle of frigid water that was steadily gathering around him, he didn't know, and he was becoming too tired to even care.

"Just tell me what the big deal is?" Oliver asked in a burst of foolish courage. "Why do you want the gem so bad?"

The crow's eyes narrowed into dark, lifeless holes as he answered. "There is only one thing in this whole stupid world that matters. It is the thing that makes others fear you, which is also the very thing that gets them to do whatever you need. That thing is—power."

"No way!" Oliver couldn't stop himself from responding. "Want to know something? I used to think that nothing mattered. But I was just as wrong as you are now."

Oliver knew the crow didn't care, but he continued anyway. "It took me a long time, but I learned it. I found it out kind of by accident. The thing that matters most—is friendship."

A sinister laugh sprang from The General's twisted beak. "Friendship?"

His tone was mocking and disgusted. "Friends are temporary. They either become your next meal, or get squashed by a truck, or caught on a hook, or crushed in a human's hand. No. It's power that rules the roost. I've been biding my time, waiting to tear apart the Alliance so that I could take control. But with your magic—I can do so much more."

"You're crazy," Oliver said, feeling the ice-cold rainwater rising around his coiled, numbing body.

"Crazy? No, silly boy. You see, I plan to use your little gem to force each and every pitiful Pond creature to become a crow."

The General was almost giddy as he relayed his plan. "Thanks to what you possess, a hive of bees will become a murder of crows! Beavers, bats, foxes, frogs—all will be crows! Crows that will do my bidding—because I will be the most powerful crow of all!"

"C-*cacacawwwwwww!*" The General's cackle unnerved Oliver so much that the tears he'd been holding back finally began to flow into the icy water that surrounded him.

"Good-bye, boy." The crow raised his beak high, ready to strike.

Oliver closed his eyes. As on TV, he expected to see his short life flash by in a kind of greatest-hits video, but instead, all he saw was an image of Mooch.

"Don't give up, Ollie. Don't let go," the salamander said. And then the image of his friend disappeared, leaving only darkness.

He opened his eyes and saw The General lunging for him. Oliver forced every ounce of his energy to move his snake body, managing to slither just far enough out of the trajectory of the attack for The General to miss him. The crow's beak splashed into the water like a misfired missile.

Oliver watched, trembling, as The General whipped around and shrieked, "*Caacawwwwwwww!* Die, boy—*die!*"

Antoine was halfway across the Pond, already feeling defeated in his search for Oliver, when The General's shout stopped him in midflight. He flipped around and raced back toward the Crag's cliffs—raced with a speed he'd never known, beating his wings against the freezing rain.

"*Caaaaw!* I'm coming, Ollie! *Cacaaaaawwww!*"

Oliver and The General heard the distant call and both recognized it immediately as Antoine's.

"What a gift, two killings for the price of one." Then The General bent down and whispered in Oliver's ear, "I'll deal with you in a minute—after I take care of a little family business."

Oliver scanned the crevice for escape routes, but there were none. It's no use, he thought. Even if I could get past The General, I'm way too weak to climb down the cliff.

He resigned himself to his fate: The General would soon be back, Antoine would most likely be dead, and then he too would be killed by the maniacal crow. Oliver sank back into the rising water. This is it, he thought. The last moments of my way-too-short life.

Oliver turned to look at his wound, and was amazed

by what he saw. The runoff from the rain continued to flow into the crevice—but the water around him was slowly going down. And with that realization, a tiny ray of hope shot through him. The water was flowing, which meant it had a place to go. A place OUT!

Oliver's spirit was suddenly light again as he saw a narrow hole where the water was disappearing.

He took a deep breath and then pushed himself into the tunnel of darkness that would, he hoped, lead him back into the light.

CHAPTER TWENTY-EIGHT

THE FREEZING RAIN continued to turn the night into a nightmare, encasing everything it touched in a thick icy glaze. Dozens of phone wires had already snapped under the frozen weight.

Driving was treacherous. It was the first storm of the season, and the town's two sand trucks weren't up and running yet. The few drivers that were either brave or stupid enough to be out, drove slowly, hoping that their vehicles would somehow stay on the road.

"*Amphibian* derives from the Greek and means 'two

249

lives.' Did you know that, salamander?" Oliver's dad said to Mooch, who was still lying on the car's rear stereo speaker.

Mooch had to smile, thinking that for him, "two lives" meant more than just life on land and in the water. He had one life as a salamander, and thanks to Oliver, had had a second one as a boy.

"You're going to like your new home," Arthur said over his shoulder. "There'll be lots of different creatures there. It'll be like camp. You know, my son went to camp."

He then remembered something. "My son hated camp."

Arthur put the wipers on high, which helped him see the yellow sign with the large S that indicated a curve. He slowed down, but as the road turned to the left, the car continued straight—smashing through a metal guardrail and disappearing into the darkness.

"Look, I believe you. It's a matter of life and death. But whose? And why did you have to involve me?" Rachel drove carefully as she tried getting Willy to explain this strange mission to her.

"I'm not exactly sure what's going to happen," the dragonfly replied from his perch atop the car's rearview mirror. "All I know is, your father has my friend. And they're both somehow in deep trouble. Or headed for it, anyway."

They drove on in silence for a few minutes. Willy wanted to tell Rachel that her brother had been captured by the large crow, but he knew that there was nothing she could do.

"I keep thinking that this is all a dream, you know?" Rachel said to Willy, whose eyes suddenly flickered wide.

"Look. Someone's gone off the road!" He was pointing ahead to the crushed guardrail and several knocked down trees. "Stop the car!"

Rachel jammed her foot on the brake. The wheels stopped, but the car didn't. Rachel and Willy screamed as her mother's car spun in circles before crashing sideways against a pine tree.

"You okay?" Willy asked from the floor.

"I think so," Rachel replied as she forced the dented car door open. "There!" She pointed to a dim light in the rain-drenched forest below them. "I see the taillights. It's my dad's car!"

Willy joined Rachel as she clambered down the steep embankment toward the car, which was dangerously close to sliding into a ravine, with Rachel's dad and Mooch trapped inside.

Antoine flew through the rain toward the rocky fortress where he hoped he'd find Oliver. He blinked the frozen water from his eyes, just barely able to see The General's ominous figure. Antoine began to tremble at the thought of confronting his uncle, but he knew it was something he had to do.

"I just want my friend," he called out bravely. "I don't want to hurt you."

"What a shame," replied The General, leaning out from the ledge. "Because I can't wait to hurt you!"

Antoine knew that he had to defend himself. He pushed his head down and darted below the oncoming attack, narrowly escaping his uncle's blow.

"Aha, so you did learn something in training!" shouted The General, almost impressed with his nephew's deft move. "But tell me, Antoine, how does one deal with *this*?"

The General swooped back around, and Antoine had no choice but to flee.

"Yes! Yes! Run away, you foolish crow!" The General was gaining now, each massive push of his wings equal to twice that of Antoine's.

"Think . . . think." Antoine searched his brain for an idea that might help him. He swerved up—The General was there. He dove toward the ground—his uncle cut him off.

"Pity that it comes down to this, isn't it, nephew?" said The General as he circled around Antoine, who hung helplessly in the wet, cold sky. "They say blood is thicker than water. What do you say we find out, hmmm?"

Antoine felt defeated. What was he thinking? He'd set out to rescue Oliver, but it looked like all he'd really done was get himself killed.

"You're weak, Antoine," The General yelled as he gained on his retreating nephew until he was just a hard bite away. "Weak and stupid. Just like your mother!"

His mother? Weak? Stupid? Antoine felt his bottled-up rage burst open. His eyes burned with hatred, and before he could think, he looped quickly up into the air and circled backward, over, and then under, into the exposed belly of his uncle.

"Arrgh! Idiot!" screamed The General as Antoine's sharp beak pierced his skin.

"Say what you want about me," Antoine shouted, wrapping his wings tightly around The General, "but leave my mother alone."

To an observer it might have looked as though Antoine and his uncle were locked in a loving midair embrace. But Antoine was using the last of his energy to pin The General's wings to his side.

The two crows began to fall from the sky as one. The General struggled to free himself, but Antoine's wings were clasped around him like a cocoon.

"Let go, fool!" shouted The General. "You'll kill us both!"

"Then at least I'll die knowing that you'll never hurt anyone ever again."

Antoine felt the rain, the wind, and as he braced for the deadly crash—he felt the sudden pain of Shadow's beak tear into his left wing, causing him to let go of The General and fall helplessly into the abyss below.

* * *

The car had slid off the ice-slicked road and rolled down the incline, knocking over small trees as it ricocheted off the boulders. It had finally stopped, just feet away from a steep drop that would no doubt be fatal.

"What can you see? Are they okay?" Rachel yelled to Willy, who'd been able to fly down to the car first.

Willy peered in through the frozen windshield, searching desperately for any signs of life. Mooch was nowhere to be seen, but Rachel's father was right in front of him, collapsed on top of the steering wheel. Willy couldn't tell if the man was breathing, and prayed that he wasn't dead.

Rachel slid on her butt down the last five feet to get to the car. "Dad? Dad! Can you hear me?" she shouted, banging her fists against the window, praying he would respond.

Inside the car, Arthur heard a muffled sound that felt like snowballs slamming dully against his head. He slowly opened his eyes.

"Dad!" Rachel shouted as soon as she saw him sit up. "Are you okay?"

She watched him nod. "I think so," Arthur groaned. "Just a couple of bruises."

Willy hovered by Rachel's face. "Ask him about Mooch. Ask him!"

"We're going to get you out of there," Rachel said as calmly as she could. "But, Dad, what happened to

Mooch—I mean the salamander? Is he still with you?"

"Salamander?" he said foggily. "I think so." Arthur tried to reach behind the front seat, but as he stretched backward, he was gripped by pain.

"Ow, my leg!"

Looking down, Rachel saw that his left leg was bent into a shape it was never designed to make. She reached for the door handle and pulled, trying to force the mangled metal free. But it only budged a crack.

"That's it! I'm going in!" yelled Willy as he flew through the tiny door opening. He zipped past Arthur's head and into the backseat, desperate for any sign of his friend.

"Mooch? Are you back here? Mooch?"

Willy's heartbeat filled a silence that seemed to last for weeks.

Finally a soft voice called out from under the front seat. "Willy? Is that you?"

The dragonfly darted down to the floor and saw the speckled face of his oldest friend poke out from the darkness.

"Dude, you okay?"

"Yeah. Fine," said the salamander. "What a wild ride!"

The distant sound of a cracking tree branch brought back the worry to Willy's face.

"I gotta tell you, Willy. It's the strangest thing; I feel like I am supposed to be here. Supposed to help, somehow."

"I know. And you did help," replied Willy, as another tree branch cracked in the distance. "If you hadn't been in the car, we wouldn't have followed, and . . . I'll explain later."

Outside, the freezing rain continued its attack on the tree limbs. Branches imprisoned in thick ice were snapping off and falling—and if the weather didn't change soon . . .

Snap! Crash! Thud!

A heavy oak branch landed on the roof of the car. Rachel screamed, not only out of fright, but because the impact of the branch made the car lurch forward—closer to the edge of the ravine.

"Willy! Hurry up!" she shouted.

Willy urged the salamander to crawl up to the front seat, while he flew back outside to Rachel.

"I have only one idea," Willy said to Rachel. "But it depends on your knowing how to work your brother's magic."

Arthur was in so much pain, he hardly noticed that his daughter was carrying on a conversation with a dragonfly. He watched as she reached inside her pocket and took out what looked like a shiny piece of glass.

"Dad, I know this is weird, but just do it, okay? For me?" There were tears in Rachel's eyes, and her voice was shaking.

Arthur was barely conscious, but he managed a thin, reassuring smile. "Sure, sweetheart. Whatever you say."

By now, Mooch had scampered up onto Arthur's lap. He watched as Willy flew back inside the narrow door opening.

"Okay, Dad, lift your hand—let the dragonfly and salamander rest in your palm."

Arthur followed her directions, picking up Mooch, then pushing his right hand toward the insect.

The slow creaking sound of another breaking branch filled the air. Rachel looked directly above and saw a heavy limb begin to bend.

"Now, touch my fingers," Rachel said, and then she pushed her left hand through the car door opening. Her thumb and forefinger held the fragment of Oliver's gem.

Above them, the branch finally separated from the tree, snapping like brittle bones. Rachel saw the limb fall toward her just as her father's pinky grazed the gem.

The branch slammed onto the hood of the car—smashing the windshield, crushing the roof, and landing on the spot where Rachel stood.

But Rachel was no longer there. Her dragonfly wings had propelled her out of the way, and she hovered above the car, thankful that the magic had worked.

Mooch was only mildly surprised to find himself a slightly pudgy dragonfly. But Arthur, already delirious with pain, simply assumed he was dreaming.

"I always wanted to fly!" he sang out.

"It worked, Willy! It worked!" Rachel cried, her new red-striped body glistening in the rain.

The three dragonflies surrounded Arthur, who by now was certain he was losing it. Rachel clung to her father's thorax and whispered, "It's going to be all right, Dad. Everything is going to be fine."

CHAPTER TWENTY-NINE

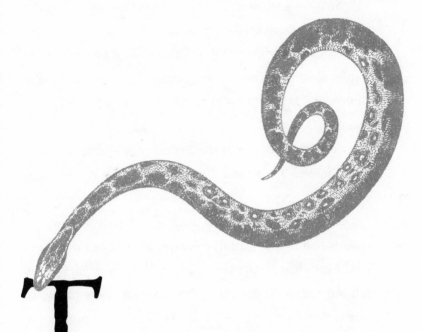

THERE WAS NO TURNING BACK. Like the water that flowed past him, Oliver had only one way to go. Where he would end up, Oliver hadn't a clue. He only knew that moving forward into the unknown was far preferable to waiting to be killed by The General.

His whole body hurt, and his eyes could see nothing but darkness, but he pushed and slithered and poked whichever way the water went. He was way beyond cold, way beyond afraid.

* * *

"Sir, you're hurt!"

Shadow gasped at The General's chest wound as the two crows landed on the icy ledge.

"It's a small price to pay for finally getting rid of my nephew." At first The General smiled, but then scowled at the cadet. "My nephew, who YOU were supposed to be guarding!"

"Um, we had a bit of trouble." Shadow gulped.

"*Trouble?* What kind of trouble?" Trouble was not part of his plan.

Embarrassed, Shadow told The General how the insects had helped Antoine escape. How they'd overpowered him, then all the crow cadets. Shadow conveniently left out the worst part: that all the insects were just kids. The General would surely find that out later, but for now, telling half the truth was about all Shadow could handle.

"*Insects? Bugs?* Defeating the crows?" The General laughed. "That is just not possible."

"I'm sorry, sir. It's that strange snake. He got them all worked up."

"*The snake!*"

Having turned his attention to killing Antoine, The General had forgotten about Oliver.

"This snake is not what he seems," began The General. He was planning to tell Shadow about the magic, and make him an ally in the secret. First, however, he needed to put Shadow to the test.

"The snake's back there. Bring him to me."

Shadow saluted dutifully and then hobbled to the crevice. But when he got there, he thought that this must be one of The General's cruel tricks. There was no snake. Just a steady flow of rainwater gathering in a pool at the base of the wall.

Shadow swallowed deeply before yelling back, "Um, he's not here, sir. That snake is gone."

"Gone?!" shouted The General as he stormed toward Shadow. "Impossible!"

His eyes were now wide open, scanning every inch of the confined space. "The snake was trapped here. There was no place for him to go! Look harder!"

Shadow scraped his beak against the wet gap in the rocks, finally finding the tiny opening where the water escaped. "General! Over here. It's a hole, sir."

"Fool! Idiot! It's all your fault!"

The General pinned Shadow against the wall, his beak inches from the cadet's chest. "Because *you* let my nephew go, *he* stopped me from killing the boy!"

Boy? thought a confused Shadow as he covered his head with his wings.

"I had such big plans for you," The General said, looking into the cadet's dimming eyes. "Good-bye, Shadow."

Inch by slow inch, Oliver wriggled through the twisted path within the Crag.

Whenever he came close to giving up, Mooch's voice would urge him on. "Get your butt home, Oliver. I want to go swimming!" In his delirious state, Oliver talked back to Mooch.

"Swimming? You call your belly-flopping mess 'swimming'?"

"Oh, you think you can do better? Then get back home and show me!" encouraged Mooch's voice.

"Home . . ." thought Oliver, so filled with longing, he wanted to just stop and cry.

But he couldn't quit. Not yet. He pushed along the watery trail until finally the tunnel straightened out into a long level stretch, which gave Oliver new strength.

He pushed himself forward, but suddenly, the tunnel disappeared. Time stopped and then gravity took over as Oliver dropped into a hole.

"Ahhh!"

As he fell through the darkness, Oliver felt like a bird again.

Splash! Oliver's limp body landed in a deep pool. After the initial shock, wiggling in the water actually felt good. But the sudden realization of *why* he'd fallen into a pool of water chilled him to the bone.

The water was deep and rising because it had nowhere else to go. This was the end of the tunnel.

The end of his life.

CHAPTER THIRTY

F A R U P the twisted maze, The General continued to use his beak and claws to widen the hole that Oliver had used to escape. He assumed that Oliver had simply managed to slither into a new hiding place on the other side of this rocky wall.

"I'm coming for you!" he screamed through the opening.

The General's stomach wound was raw, and his beak was scraped and bent—and still he picked and poked and broke his way through the rock.

Ready to go in for the kill, The General backed up and took a deep breath before running full throttle toward the hole.

The impact was loud—a painful, head-to-rock crack that filled the dead air. Larger pieces of rock broke away.

The General pushed his head and shoulders through, positive that the cowering snake would be right there on the other side.

But there was no snake. Just a steady stream of water flowing past him that disappeared down a tunnel; a tunnel perfect for a snake but much too narrow for him.

"This isn't over yet, boy!" The General yelled, and then he shrieked at the top of his lungs. "*Cacawwwww!*"

His loud cry boomed within the rocky cavern.

Then the echo of his call was followed by a rumbling groan that gave him one shocking moment to realize what was happening. He had caused an avalanche.

He shrieked as the wall and ceiling cracked then collapsed on top of him.

The only evidence of General Eduardo Ignatio Santo Domingo's reign of terror was the bent tip of his beak that peeked up from his stony grave.

It had been a minute since Oliver's final breath, and now, as he floated closer to the end, he realized he could no longer feel his body. Though the water was frigid, he was filled with a warmth that oddly reminded him of taking a bath when he was a kid.

And as he let go of the terror inside and began to sink slowly, Oliver thought he could hear a rumbling sound like a thundering waterfall.

The General's avalanche had released a powerful surge of water that roared down the tunnel and exploded into the cavern, spinning Oliver with it.

The pounding flood pressed against the rock wall. The pressure built quickly, and then the wall gave up—crumbling like a sandcastle at high tide.

Oliver was on the edge of consciousness as a strong swift current burst from the rocks, propelling his snake body away from the cliffs, over the trees, past the reeds and rushes, and into the shallows of the Pond.

He landed with a hard *slap* and became instantly aware that his body was no longer numb. Groaning with the pain of a belly flop, he had to smile. He was alive.

As the freezing rain finally slowed, then stopped altogether, Oliver used the last of his energy to wiggle onto the pebbled shore. Looking up he saw a vision so spectacular, it scared him into thinking he might actually be dead.

The first glimmer of sunrise tore the gray clouds open, and as Oliver focused, he was greeted by a world that sparkled and shined. Everything—trees and rocks and blades of grass—were glistening in ice.

To Oliver, the entire world was glowing just like his

precious gem. He looked again at the sparkling Pond, at the jewels all around him. And then he passed out, finally resting with inner sense that everything was going to be all right.

"Oliver? Oliver . . ." A voice was whispering from a far-off place. But it was so far away, it was barely audible. "O-li-ver?"

The hazy veil inside his head slowly began to lift, and Oliver became aware of a familiar voice.

"Come on, Oliver. Wake up."

All he wanted was to sleep. But the voice wouldn't stop calling.

"Ollie? You back, man?"

Slowly, Oliver opened his eyes and saw the dark silhouette in front of him. It was a grinning crow.

"Antoine! You're alive!" He sat up quickly, then reached out and hugged his friend.

"Ow, the wing. Watch the wing."

Oliver saw that Antoine's wing was broken again. He touched the mangled twist of feather and bone. Then he saw his own stubby fingers and realized all at once that he was no longer a snake.

"I'm me! I'm me again!"

"Yeah, you're you. And he's him. And you're both pretty lucky to be alive."

Oliver turned around and saw Reggie, the garbage crow grinning next to several of his mangy crew. "Don't mean to brag—but Antoine here's lucky we found him when we did. We found him. He found you."

"I don't understand. The General? The fight? What happened, exactly? I'm not sure how much I remember or how much I dreamed."

They told him about the wild crow battle in the sky; about Antoine's terrible fall, where he was lucky to land on the trees, not rocks; about Hinky, guilt-ridden and desperate, going back to the garbage dump and asking for help; and how Reggie led his ragged bunch through the rain-soaked sky, searching endlessly for Antoine, for Oliver, for any lingering crow cadets who needed one more reminder that they were no longer welcome at the Pond.

"By the way, kid, lemme know when you wanna eat like a crow again. I got some fresh maggots back at the dump with your name on 'em."

Oliver laughed. "Thanks, Reggie, but if it's all the same—I think I'll stick with this body for a while."

They all smiled nervously. They were glad Oliver was feeling all right. He had made it to the end of a terrifying journey in one piece. Well, almost, anyway, because no one, not even Antoine, had the heart to tell him—he was missing his left foot.

CHAPTER THIRTY-ONE

T HE POND was frozen over into a thick mirror of the wintry sky. The naked autumn trees and stark, still woods had been transformed by the blanket of snow that had fallen before Thanksgiving. Squirrels burrowed into empty logs and tree trunks; frogs hid underwater, fast asleep in the deep cool mud. Even slugs and worms found underground hiding places that kept them safely hidden from winter's frozen touch.

Back in Little Falls, Belinda Shrank felt just awful for the family on No-way Way. Moved all the way here to start over—and then so many dreadful things happened at once. She couldn't shake the thought that the ugly house was cursed somehow.

But business was business, and she suspected that the house would soon be back on the market. There'd be no way that family would stay now, not with all they'd been through.

First there was the ex-husband's car accident, leaving him with a broken hip and leg and stuck in a dreadful body cast. How he'd dragged himself all the way from the crash, six miles to the hospital, no one knew. Funny, how they'd found him, too, lying outside by the Emergency Room entrance, going on about his wings.

And then there was that poor boy. Lost in the woods during the same terrible ice storm. Could've happened to anybody. And what a shame about his foot. Stepped in a fox trap—took the thing clear off.

Belinda turned the van onto the dirt road with a big bump that spilled hot tuna noodle casserole onto her son's lap.

"I don't see why you had to drag me along," Brody Shrank complained to his mother, who seemed even more nervous than usual.

"The girl is in your class. It's neighborly."

"It's stupid," was his reply, as he scooped up the glop of casserole from his jeans and stuffed it into his mouth.

* * *

"Really, Cherise—for the zillionth time—it's okay." Rachel was on the couch sipping hot chocolate, the phone cradled against her ear. Cherise had been calling two, sometimes three times a day to make sure Rachel was all right; that their friendship wasn't damaged because she'd confessed the whole plan to Rachel's mom.

"Yeah, we got punished for the lying, sneaking out, car-stealing thing. But the end result was worth it. And you did exactly what you were supposed to do—even telling my mom. You were amazing! The best friend ever."

Carol carried in a bowl of soup and placed it on the wooden table by the fire where Arthur sat, encased in his cast.

"I can't thank you enough," he said. His entire left side, from shoulder to big toe, was covered in a long hard cast.

"Arthur, there's no way I was going to let you try to manage alone in the city. You've been through a lot."

The truth was, they'd all been through a lot. Accepting the two horrible accidents was difficult. But both parents had to also come to grips with what had saved father and son: the magic of the gem.

"Aha! It *did* happen!" Arthur had shouted when he was told the details of his rescue. He was relieved that his strange memory of being a dragonfly hadn't been a dream.

Carol, always the scientist, was more skeptical. But once she was shown proof, by being transformed into a cockroach, she had to accept the magic—*and* just how dirty it was behind her stove.

The loud knock on the front door surprised them all. They weren't expecting visitors; in fact, these days they did their best to keep people away. Rachel looked to her mother, who nodded her consent.

"Someone's here, gotta go." Rachel finished her good-bye to Cherise as she got up and opened the door. She was shocked to see the doughy face of Brody Shrank and his jittery mother.

"Do us a little favor, honey?" Belinda's eye had begun to twitch. "Let us in before that fella over there gets any ideas."

Rachel looked past the guests and saw the one-eyed glare of Hinky, who had made it his full-time job to guard and protect the little house.

"Belinda, what a surprise. Come in." Carol ushered them inside. Belinda sighed with relief.

Rachel still felt queasy whenever she was near Brody. Her brief time as a captured frog in his beefy hands was something she'd never forget. Fortunately, all she had to do to regain her self-respect was remember how she'd used his head as a toilet.

Belinda's goal was simple: show up, make nice, find out when they'd be moving, and get them to list the house with her. She'd find them another house, and maybe, finaly get this one demolished. She hated being in that house, and hoped to be back inside her van in eight, maybe ten minutes, max.

"Sell the place?" Carol was so surprised, she actually laughed. "Why would I do that?"

"Oh, well, I just thought with all the bad luck and all." Belinda was caught in her own trap. "Maybe living out here just wasn't right for you. Icky bugs, crazy birds, smelly animals."

"Ahhhhh!"

Brody jumped from his chair as if something had suddenly bitten him on the butt. In fact, he had been bitten on the butt—by two dozen red ants.

"Nice work, guys," yelled their commander. "Next time, don't forget the ankles!"

As Brody ran to his mother's side, a fat frog jumped onto Belinda's head, croaking and farting at the same time.

"Not again," Belinda moaned, frozen in terror. Reggie, the garbage crow, flew in from the kitchen and dropped banana peels on Brody and a nice shower of coffee grounds on Belinda. Brody began to tremble, and Rachel and her father had to work hard to stifle a laugh.

"Now do you see what I've been saying about this house?" Belinda whimpered to her son.

The deafening *rat-a-tat-tat* of a woodpecker banged wildly away on a wood beam above them. Belinda and Brody looked up, startled—and slipped on the banana peels.

"Funny thing is," Carol said, "this house suits us just fine."

Rachel held the front door wide open, and the real

estate agent and her son scrambled to get outside, doing their best to avoid the dozens of tiny spiders that were now dropping from the ceiling like bungee-corded daredevils.

Thanks to Brody, who had accidentally left the van door slightly open, Hinky had left them with a wonderful gift: a skunky smell that would stay in the car for many years to come.

Rachel was laughing so hard, tears streamed down her cheeks. And even though the slightest chuckle made her father's body feel as though it was being torn in half, he too was giggling.

"That was pretty good," Carol said. She stood by the fire, suddenly a little sad. "There was only one thing missing."

And everyone—bird, bug, and sister alike—had to agree: it was too bad Oliver couldn't have been there to see it.

CHAPTER THIRTY-TWO

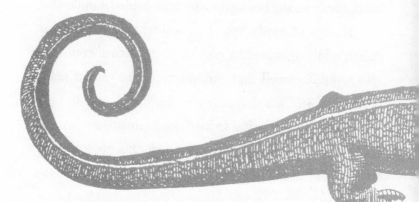

OLIVER'S ROOM was pretty much the same, except cleaner. There were no dirty clothes to put away. No need to change the sheets on a bed never slept in. It was as though no one had used the room for months, which actually was kind of true.

Of course, Oliver hadn't lost his foot to a fox trap. But some alternate explanation for his missing appendage was needed, and no sane person would believe what had really happened. So Carol purposely planted the story with a gossipy waitress at the diner.

The truth was, when Oliver had been a snake, The General had pierced his tail. The wound was so bad that, when he became a boy again—he was a boy without a foot.

"No fair. I want to watch Oprah!"

Antoine rattled his cage. He hated the fact that his wing was back in a sling. He couldn't use the remote. He turned to the wallet-sized school photo of Cherise taped to his bars and lamented, "Why me, sugar? Why me?"

"Tough break, tough guy," Mooch called from his glass tank, the TV remote under his front legs. "I'm learning how to make fondue!"

The TV sat on Oliver's old desk. On the program, a rotund woman was preparing a vat of warm chocolate.

"Mmm. I'd give anything to be dipped in that!" said Mooch.

"Tell you what," a nearby voice said. "Another month or two, and I'll grant that wish."

Mooch turned and smiled. Oliver may have lost a foot, but his sense of humor was intact—even as a salamander.

"Ollie, dude, get him to change channels. Puleeease?" whined Antoine.

Oliver just shook his amphibian head. "Sorry, Antoine. Mooch and I may be roommates, but the TV stuff is between you two. Besides, I have tons of homework."

Oliver took a sip from his water dish and then went back to reading the tiny version of his history textbook;

one of the many mini-schoolbooks his mother had painstakingly made for him at the copy store. He was glad he didn't have to fall too far behind at school, but still wished he could just lay back and enjoy the time in his temporary salamander body.

The idea had actually come from Mooch: if salamanders can naturally regenerate missing limbs and tails, why couldn't Oliver regrow his foot? "Of course, you're gonna have to be a salamander again. Think you can handle it?"

It was the first time the boy had smiled since the accident.

In the six short weeks he'd been inside the glass tank, evidence of growth had begun. Cells had been slowly gathering and building, giving Oliver hope that he would once again have toes to wiggle in the sand.

His mother charted the growth with careful measurements, while his father was busy writing a research article on the relationship between regeneration and prosthetics. But Oliver didn't care about furthering science. All he wanted was to walk again.

"Knock-knock." His mother was carrying a tray with treats for all three friends—hamburger bits, small bowls of soda, teeny French fries.

"By the way, guys, no more TV. It's time for visiting hours."

She reached over, unplugged the television, and left, as

Oliver, Mooch, and Antoine saw the familiar blur of Willy's blue wings flutter into the room.

"Yo, dudes!" the dragonfly called out, landing on the rim of the glass tank. "I brought you guys a surprise."

"Some fresh flies?" asked Mooch.

"The answers to my history test?" said Oliver.

"Cherise?" moaned Antoine.

"No. Me." The voice belonged to the head of the Pond Alliance, the black widow spider whose leadership had nearly come to a deadly end. Fat Mama used her silken string to climb atop the tank, where she settled next to Willy.

"We haven't officially met," the spider said to Oliver, "but our paths have crossed."

Fat Mama smiled, then dropped onto the gravel and walked to Oliver's side.

"So many things happen in a lifetime. It's often hard to see that each event is linked together and that nothing happens that doesn't somehow touch something else."

Oliver looked at his friends. The pudgy salamander, the wild crow, the proud dragonfly—they were all kids who didn't quite fit in, just like him. He felt connected to them. Is that what she meant?

"Life is like a web. Each of us—spider or squirrel, fish or boy—we spin a web, a web made up of every moment we live and breathe. Good things. Terrible things. Nothing ever happens that is truly wrong, because even then, it is connected to the chance to make things right."

Oliver closed his eyes and saw all the threads that formed his own web. His parents' divorce; his lonely life in his room; moving to the new house; accidentally finding the gem; Mooch; flying with Antoine; a renewed bond with Rachel; and his battle against The General. So many things—good and bad—all woven together.

"There is one more thing," she called out as she climbed out of the tank. "I want you all to meet the newest member of the Alliance."

All eyes looked up expectantly. Antoine was especially curious to see who would be picked to replace his evil uncle. But oddly—no one entered the room. The spider grinned.

"The newest member of the Alliance is Willy."

"Me?" the dragonfly said. "But I'm a kid."

"You are a member of the Pond," Fat Mama said. "And I apologize that it has taken this old spider so long to see that every voice needs to be heard. You have shown more than good leadership; you have been a good friend."

Willy's wings buzzed into a humming blur as he circled the room shouting, "Did you hear that? I'm in the Alliance! For real! Yee-ha!!"

Mooch and Oliver cheered, and Antoine rattled his beak against the metal bars. Now kids from all the species would have a say in what went on at the Pond.

"It's about time," shouted Mooch. "Way to go, Willy!"

Fat Mama excused herself. She looked forward to seeing Oliver back on his boy feet soon. "And I expect to see you tomorrow night, Willy. It's the New Moon Meeting of the Alliance."

And then she was gone, floating out the window on a golden thread.

"Oh, man. Is this awesome or what?!" Antoine called out to his friends. He was pumped and proud, and did the only thing he could think of. He started making some noise.

"*Cacaw, chchcaw, Cacacaw, chchcaaaaw . . .*"

The pumping beat filled the room and then burst into a song, a song they all sang together.

"We wanna, wanna, wanna be big fat green iguanas! Fly above the clouds, we wanna! Singing songs all day! We wanna, wanna, wanna, watch the sun set on the water! We really wanna really be good friends always."

CHAPTER THIRTY-THREE

MARCH is an unpredictable month. It's the month when anything can happen—a freakish three-foot snowstorm or a sudden thaw that gives the first crocus a chance to poke through a melting layer of ice.

March was also the month when Oliver was able to return to school. According to his mother's meticulous measurements, the regeneration was complete. The new foot had remained the same size for two weeks, and even though it was slightly smaller than the other, both parents agreed—the experiment was finished.

The night before school, the family threw a "Going Away/Welcome Back" party for Oliver and his bedroom companions. Rachel led Oliver into the room blindfolded. His new foot was still weak, and he limped just slightly.

"Okay, Ollie, you can lift off the blindfold on the count of three," Rachel called out. "One, two . . ."

"Three!" A gaggle of voices all shouted at once.

Oliver whipped off the blindfold and was shocked to see a room filled with people. People he wasn't sure he even knew.

"Surprised?"

Oliver turned and saw a boy next to him. A boy he immediately recognized as Mooch.

"Long time no see, huh, pal?" said Mooch, giving his buddy a warm high five. "Welcome home, Oliver."

Oliver looked at the guests again and then recognized them all. There was crazy Antoine flirting with Cherise. The large, tough-looking guy picking delicacies from the trash would be Reggie. The bunch of leeches, who had once sucked his blood, were now in human form, guzzling whole cans of soda in one gulp. And the older woman talking to his mom, the one with the long silken black-gray hair, had to be Fat Mama, and ironically—she wasn't fat. They all were there: Hinky (who really should've taken a bath), Lester Biggs, Roxanne— all there to welcome him back. And all there as people!

Oliver went through the room, hugging, high-fiving, and thanking everyone. They treated him like a hero for foiling The General's plot which would have hurt them all.

"The thing is," a squat, wart-faced man croaked while grabbing Oliver by the shoulder, "you humans ain't so bad, you know?"

"Not all of us," said Oliver, trying to avoid the spit that sprayed from his slobbering mouth.

The blob of a man squeezed Oliver's hand in a clammy hold. "You always have a friend in Frankie, got that?"

Wandering among the guests, Oliver overheard his father having a heated debate with Dr. Kym, who was making a pretty solid case for why roadkill is a good source of protein. And passing an older, blue-haired couple on the couch, Oliver was about to introduce himself, but one whiff of their argument convinced him otherwise.

"Hey, birdbrain, I said milk," complained the woman holding out her coffee cup.

"I distinctly heard cream, Doris."

"Hello? My figure? Milk, Max. *Milk!*"

Mooch quickly pulled Oliver away. "We all pretty much steer clear of the blue jays. Crazy as loons."

"I heard that," the skinny, long-necked woman shouted from the couch. "We're *not* crazy!"

"Sorry!" Oliver and Mooch called back—then broke out laughing.

Mooch waved to Antoine, who reluctantly left Cherise's side. "I was getting somewhere, man. This better be important."

"It is," said another voice.

Oliver turned to see that a fourth boy had joined them. He was slender and had the kind of vibrant energy that suggested he could do anything—or at least he'd try.

"Willy?" Oliver had never met the dragonfly as a boy, but he recognized his bright eyes instantly.

"Not bad for a bunch of outcasts, huh?" Willy said, grabbing the other three friends around the shoulders. "We did pretty good."

"*Pretty good?*" asked Antoine. "I'd say awesome!"

Mooch pointed to Oliver's foot. "Must feel great to be back to normal."

Back to normal. Oliver had never felt normal, so it wasn't a place he'd even recognize. Tomorrow he had to go to school, where he'd feel like a stranger and a target. Unfortunately, *that* was the normal he was going back to.

"Hey, wouldn't it be great if we could stay like this?" Oliver said. "You know, us four as guys? Always?"

Antoine looked over at Cherise. "Count me in. I'm all over that!"

"Whoa. Smooth your feathers," Willy said. "I'm sorry, Oliver, but you know we don't belong here."

"But I don't make friends," Oliver said. "With you guys it was so easy."

Oliver turned to Mooch, hoping he'd back him up. But Mooch just looked away.

"You made friends in our world," Willy said. "You can do that in yours too. Trust me."

If it hadn't been a school night, the party surely would have gone on until dawn. But the time soon came, and one by one the guests left their human forms—and left the house.

Outside, Oliver and Mooch sat on the creaky front steps. It was an early spring night; still chilly, but full of the promise of things to come.

"You were pretty quiet inside," Oliver said, as he watched Mooch wolf down one last piece of cake.

Mooch wiped the frosting off his face with his shirt-sleeve. "Ollie, this is kind of tough, but . . ."

"I know. You're moving out on me." Oliver laughed. "Duh. You think it's normal for a salamander to live in a stinky old fish tank?"

"Normal? No. But the best thing that ever happened to me? Absolutely!"

The two boys hugged good-bye, hiding the tears they both were too embarrassed to show.

"See ya around, Mooch."

"You can count on it, Ollie."

Mooch closed his eyes and took a deep breath. A gentle breeze whispered past them both, and then—the boy was gone and in his place stood the plump spotted salamander, a tiny smear of vanilla frosting on his mouth.

Oliver watched Mooch walk toward the Pond, taking the path back to his own life. And as soon as he could no longer see his salamander friend, Oliver turned and walked back into his life too.

284